For the first . . . **to Hope, Di**x **. . . wasn't eager** . . .

What a difference a mere twenty-four hours made.

No, that wasn't quite right. It was the man seated across the table from her who could claim sole responsibility for her sudden discontent. This attractive, bossy, and refreshingly gallant man had shown her how empty her life really was.

Suddenly, she wasn't as eager to discover the secret as she had been when she'd arrived. Her and Mark's common goal of finding out the truth allowed her to spend time with the handsome doctor and every day's delay meant one more day in Hope. One more day of dreaming that she wasn't alone.

She'd almost be willing to let something develop between them, but fear held her back. In spite of her faith in her family, deep down she was afraid that it might be misplaced. And if it was, any relationship she developed with Mark in the interim would wither after the painful truth was revealed.

Dear Reader

Welcome to my HOPE CITY series, where people find love as they pursue their dreams and aspirations.

The idea for this series grew out of the knowledge that we've all entertained hopes at one time or another. So I wanted to create a town where my characters not only give hope to others through their profession, but, for various reasons, also cling to it themselves.

The GP's Valentine Proposal is the third story, where the discovery of a huge family secret by Dr Dixie Albright leads to her very own perfect proposal from fellow practitioner Dr Mark Cameron! Look for Hope City Hospital's other gorgeous doctor, Justin St. James, in the next story, where the combination of medicine and romance gives the community its name.

Happy reading!

Jessica Matthews

THE GP'S VALENTINE PROPOSAL

BY
JESSICA MATTHEWS

MILLS & BOON®

First published in Great Britain 2004
Paperback edition 2005
Harlequin Mills & Boon Limited,
Eton House, 18-24 Paradise Road, Richmond, Surrey TW9 1SR

© Jessica Matthews 2004

ISBN 0 263 84287 8

Set in Times Roman 10¼ on 11 pt.
03-0205-55733

Printed and bound in Spain
by Litografía Rosés, S.A., Barcelona

CHAPTER ONE

"WHAT do you think you're doing?"

Startled by the irritated male voice that had come from nowhere, Dixie Albright jumped and banged her injured knee on the open drawer. Pain shot through her leg to the point of instantly bringing tears to her eyes, but she managed to swallow both her groan and a few choice words.

"Well?" he demanded as he strode into the office and hovered over the oak desk like an avenging angel.

She didn't need this, she decided as she took a few bracing breaths. She didn't need to undo the surgeon's work so soon after he'd repaired the damage, and she certainly didn't need to be treated as if she had no right to be there. Hoping to avoid this very situation, she'd checked in with Jane, the practice receptionist, who obviously hadn't spread the word about Dixie's presence.

Actually, there shouldn't have been anyone to tell. She'd arrived during the noon hour when everyone—other than Jane—had left for lunch. She'd planned to take advantage of the near-deserted practice to scout out the situation before anyone—namely her cousin's boss—realized she'd been there.

And from Ned's description, the man glowering at her could only be the top man in this three-physician family practice. As she rubbed her knee and mentally willed the pain down to a manageable level, she wondered if he always took a short lunch-break.

He probably did, she told herself. Ned had complained of his partner's workaholic tendencies, and at the time she'd hoped they'd rub off on her free-spirited cousin. Considering that she was sitting at Ned's desk in a busy medical practice while Ned was off doing only heaven knew what, those traits clearly hadn't made any impression on him.

Determined to be polite and not alienate the one man who could possibly help her, she pasted on a smile and carefully balanced her weight on her good leg as she rose and straightened out a few wrinkles on her blue Paisley skirt. Dresses weren't her favorite things to wear during the cold days of January, but pulling a pair of slacks her swollen knee seemed more work than it was worth.

"Hi," she said brightly as she held out her hand, taking stock of the impeccably dressed man who loomed over her. "You must be Mark Cameron."

While she waited for him to shake hands, she quickly created a mental list of his characteristics. Wide shoulders, powerful arms, which the long sleeves of his navy blue shirt didn't disguise, slightly windblown auburn hair, a handsome face with faint scars above his right eyebrow and along the right side of his jaw, a heart-stopping dimple in his firm chin, and gray eyes that, at the moment, were as frosty as the winter weather.

"Yes, I am. And you are?" He raised a dark eyebrow.

A lesser woman might have quaked in her boots under the circumstances, but Dixie hadn't survived medical school without weathering all sorts of situations. She'd learned how to handle bad-mannered, obnoxious, and arrogant professors by not backing down. Now, thanks to Father Time and the years under her proverbial belt—not to mention the initials after her own name—she no longer humbly accepted whatever dish a colleague tried to serve.

She shot him one of her own "doctor" glares that she saved for rare occasions, then dropped her hand and sat down. If she had to deal with rudeness, she'd do it as comfortably as possible.

"I'm Dixie…" Her comment faded as she caught a glimpse of something shiny under a pile of notepads sporting logos of various pharmaceutical companies. Distracted by the possibility of finding the very thing she'd been searching for, the very thing she *needed*, her introduction died as she grabbed for what she hoped was her prize.

It was.

Clutching the keyring like a lifeline, she sank back in the chair and sent up a silent "thank you" for her success. Without those keys, she'd be forced to call a locksmith and heaven only knew how long it would take for him to work his magic.

"You can't imagine how happy I am that I found these." She jingled them for emphasis.

"I can guess," he said dryly. A fraction of a second later, he leaned across the desk and grabbed them with a sleight of hand that would have made a magician envious. Before she truly realized what had happened and could protest, he dropped them into his trouser pocket.

She stared at him, incredulous. "What do you think you're doing?"

His expression matched his grim tone. "I asked you first."

"I've been looking for those," she ground out, struggling to contain her temper.

"You may have found them, but be glad they're in my pocket instead of yours."

"Really? Why?"

"Because if you carry those keys out of this building, I'll have you arrested for theft. Miss…?"

Her goodwill faded, along with the smile on her face. "I'm Dixie Albright and, for the record, I'm not stealing them."

"From where I stand, it looks like you are."

She gritted her teeth. "I need those keys."

He crossed his arms as a smug look crossed his face. "And why should I give them to *you*, Miss Albright?"

"It's *Dr* Albright," she said, matching his frosty tone. "As I've already explained to your receptionist, I'm Ned's cousin."

She hadn't expected him to greet her with open arms, but she *had* expected the information to soften him a bit. A blush or a sheepish smile would have suited her just fine, but all she got was a raised eyebrow. "I'm here to—" she began.

"Do you have ID?"

"To prove that I'm a physician or Ned's cousin?" she retorted.

"If you think I'm handing over *anything* to *anyone* who claims to be a relative, you can think again."

"For the love of—" She bit back the rest of her sentence. Obviously, Ned hadn't mentioned her, which pained her more than it should have. After all these years, she should be used to being invisible in his eyes. That was, she was invisible until he or his parents needed her to bail him out of the messes he landed in from time to time.

Like now.

If she weren't so tired from driving four hours and if her knee didn't throb in time to her heartbeat, she'd be relieved to know that Mark's tenacity to guard Ned's property resembled a pit bull's, but she *was* exhausted and her knee was protesting the strain. The sooner he recognized her legitimate claim to those keys, the sooner she could elevate her leg, take a pain pill and plan her next move.

Bowing to the inevitable, she fished her driver's license out of the shoulder-bag at her feet, and placed the laminated card on the polished surface of the desk.

His gaze darted to the photo ID, then back at her.

"As for being Ned's cousin..." she flipped through the snapshots in her billfold until she found the last family photo they'd taken "...will this convince you?"

He took the single photo she held out, studied the likeness, then glanced back at her. "You've changed."

"It's called age," she said smartly. A lot had happened in the six years since the photographer had snapped the picture. She'd completed her residency in emergency medicine, her uncle had died, her aunt's health had deteriorated, and her cousin...well, Ned may have finished at the top of his med-school class and specialized in family practice, but Ned was still Ned.

"That was taken six or seven years ago. I may look different, but Ned doesn't."

"You cut your hair."

She'd also exchanged her glasses for contacts with the hope that she'd undergo LASIK eye surgery one day, but he didn't need to know her medical history. "It's still me."

He handed her billfold back to her. "Why are you here?"

Dixie stuffed her belongings back in her bag before she stared at him, incredulous. "Why am I here?" she repeated.

"Ned's gone," he said flatly. "If you came to visit, you'll be sorely disappointed."

"I didn't come to visit," she said slowly. "I came to *find* him."

He scoffed. "Good luck."

Her hope that he might have a clue as to Ned's whereabouts faded. "Then you don't know where he went?"

"If I did, I'd mail his termination letter."

The situation was worse than she'd thought although, if the truth were known, not completely surprising. Ned was the type of man who marched to a different drummer, a man who played by his own rules, the most important being that he *had* no rules. Ned did what he wanted, when he wanted and somehow Dixie usually landed in the position of controlling the damage. His parents had raised her after hers had died and she, being the older of the two children in their home, had always been charged with looking out for Ned.

It was a thankless job but hers, nonetheless.

"You'd fire him because he took a vacation?" It rankled her to defend Ned when it was clear that this time he'd overextended his latest spur-of-the-moment trip, but what choice did she have?

"Disappearing without a word of warning in the middle of influenza season, leaving me high and dry with no idea of when he might come back or where he even *went*, is not the usual way to arrange for a vacation."

Dixie inwardly winced at her cousin's thoughtlessness. She didn't blame Mark for his hard-line attitude. As many faults as her cousin had, disappearing for this long exceeded even *his* limits.

Or so she hoped.

"Aren't there three of you?" she asked. "I distinctly remember Ned saying he would be the third physician in this practice."

"He was, until Don Richmond retired two months after Ned arrived. For the last three months, it's just been the two of us."

She didn't need him to spell out the obvious. To add to their already overly full schedule, Cameron had been carrying the load for the last ten days completely on his own. He had every right to be upset and less than forgiving.

What in the world were you thinking, Ned, to put your partner in this position?

"Haven't you heard from him at all?" she asked.

He snorted. "Like I told your aunt, other than the note waiting on my desk saying he'd be gone for a long weekend and a phone call that raised more questions than gave answers—"

"He called you?"

"A week later."

"What did he say? How did he sound?"

"He only said that he ran into problems and wouldn't be back for a while."

"How long?" she demanded. This was better news than she'd expected.

"The connection was bad and that was all I heard."

"Did he say what kind of problems or where he was?"

He shook his head. "It was a one-sentence conversation that basically told me nothing. So, if you should see or talk to him, tell him not to bother coming back."

She didn't think it likely that Ned would contact her. His own mother hadn't discovered he had left town until she'd phoned the practice to talk to him. Her call had been routed to Mark who, in turn, had mentioned Ned's delayed absence. As a result, her aunt had insisted on filing a missing person's report, but the police hadn't been helpful. With Ned's note and no indications of foul play, the authorities had decided that he'd disappeared by choice. Still worried about her son, her aunt had insisted on Dixie's help to discover where Ned had gone. Now, finding him was up to her, and so far Ned's phone call to Mark was her only lead.

"Aren't you being rather hasty? He might have a legitimate reason for not returning when he said he would. He could have been in a car accident, gotten ill, maybe even—"

"Ned has twenty thousand excuses but, regardless of the number, I have a three-strikes-and-you're-out policy. As far as I'm concerned, Ned's used all of his pitches. He's been permanently benched and, in fact, is off the team. End of story."

A sick feeling settled in the pit of Dixie's stomach. "Then he's done this before?" Dammit, he'd *promised* her he'd settle down after his father died, if for no other reason than to not worry his mother.

"Twice. Oh, he only left for a few days each time, but I need someone I can count on—someone the patients can count on—and clearly Ned isn't that person. So, if you've come to talk me into holding his position for the day when he may waltz back in as if nothing has happened, you're wasting your time."

Her face warmed at Cameron's uncanny accuracy. "Have you already replaced him?"

"Not yet, but I'm working on it."

"A locum?"

"For now."

"When will he or she arrive?"

He raised an eyebrow. "Does it matter?"

Her mind raced with possibilities. "Yes."

"Why?"

"Because I'm on leave for a few weeks and could fill in if you'd like. Especially since you clearly haven't replaced the fellow who retired."

"You?"

She squared her shoulders. "I'm fully qualified. As you know, family practice rotations are part of my ER training."

His gaze traveled to the crutch propped against the desk. "You're obviously not in peak condition."

"I'm only temporarily disabled," she corrected.

He didn't appear convinced and she decided to explain. "I had a meniscectomy a few days ago," she said, referring to the procedure where a piece of cartilage was removed via arthroscopy. "It was all simple and straightforward. If this personal problem hadn't come up, I'd be going back to work at home. Which means that if my orthopedist approved me to return to the ER, I can handle the demands of a family practice."

His expression grew thoughtful, and then a knowing glint appeared in his eyes. "If I let you cover for your cousin, are you assuming I'll take him back without question when he finally shows up?"

Once again, Mark had second-guessed her plan. The sneer in his voice clearly said that he found it wanting.

She met his gaze without blinking. "It's a viable idea."

"It would be," he agreed, "if I was willing to give him another chance. I'm not."

The hard set to his jaw provided ample evidence that he wouldn't be moved. Perhaps if she wasn't so tired and if her body wasn't demanding a pain pill, she'd be willing to argue Ned's case, but tomorrow, as the saying went, was another day. She wasn't ready to admit defeat, but in some instances retreating and regrouping were far better tactics to employ. This seemed like one of those times.

"I'll be staying at Ned's place until the end of the week. Provided you give me his keys," she added pointedly. "You can reach me there, in case you have second thoughts."

"I won't. My locum will arrive day after tomorrow. I have everything under control."

It didn't take much for her to imagine *no thanks to Ned* tacked onto the end of his sentence. And yet she had to put forth one final effort before she left…

"And a permanent replacement?" she asked. "For both Ned and your retired physician?"

"I'll interview my applicants in the next few weeks," he answered. "The locum will stay until I have a replacement. Everything is falling into place."

And that was that, she thought wearily.

She held out her hand. "In that case, if you don't mind, I'd like my, er, Ned's keys."

This time he didn't hesitate. He dug in his pocket and immediately dropped them into her outstretched palm. She closed her fingers around the small pieces of metal, surprised to feel how warm they had become after resting against his body, then slipped them into her skirt pocket.

"I'd also like to come back tomorrow to clear out Ned's desk." Once again, she looked him in the eye and mentally dared him to deny her request.

He didn't. "Be my guest. Someone's usually here at eight o'clock to unlock the doors, but we don't officially start until nine."

He sounded matter-of-fact, so Dixie assumed he was simply being helpful rather than implying that he wanted her in and out before his patients arrived. Little did he know that she didn't plan to dump everything in a box and haul it home. For one thing, she couldn't carry a lot and, for another, she *wanted* to run into people who knew Ned and might shed some light on where he'd gone. If the locum wouldn't arrive for forty-eight hours, she intended to spend as many of those hours in this office as possible.

"I'll keep that in mind," she said. "How much of this is his?"

"Everything, except the furniture."

She eyed the room. The bookcase lining one wall was filled with medical textbooks, magazines and newsletters. Although she hadn't identified everything in his desk, her first glance had revealed drawers crammed with an assortment of items from bottles of aspirin to throat lozenges with zinc. If that weren't enough, notebooks, notepads, tons of tourist brochures, and folders of more paper added to the variety. All in all, there was more than enough to keep her busy for days while she looked for a clue buried somewhere in this mess.

"I'll ask Jane to find some boxes for you," he said.

"Thanks."

He hesitated at the door. "If you need help…"

"Not at the moment."

"Yell if you do."

Surprised by his gruff offer, which was probably as close to an olive branch as she would receive, she nodded. "I will."

As soon as he left, she popped one of her pain pills into her mouth, swallowed it with a gulp of water from the bottle she'd bought at the convenience store when she'd arrived in Hope, and propped her leg on a chair she'd pulled toward the desk. If Ned was getting the proverbial boot to his backside, then every second she spent in this practice counted.

Hoping to find a lead in his month-at-a-glance appointment book, she flipped to the January tab and stared at the page. Other than Aunt Cora's birthday on the fifth and a dentist appointment on the eighth, the squares were eerily blank.

Where in the world are you, Ned?

Trouble. With a capital T. That's what he had in more ways than one, Mark thought as he sank into the padded executive chair behind his walnut desk.

Not only was Ned gone during the height of the viral illness season, but he himself had stretched the truth about Ned's replacement. He'd contacted the locum agency and was waiting to hear if they could accommodate his request. He'd already been warned that the firm's staff was stretched quite thin with the influenza outbreak all over the country. He didn't have a good chance of hiring a short-term physician, but they'd promised to do their best, which was all he could ask.

As for interviewing candidates for both available medical staff positions, he'd only received a single nibble for his advertising trouble. That, too, wouldn't have been so awful if the applicant had shown some potential. The man had made more demands than concessions, and even if Mark had ignored his instincts and invited him to join his practice, he had the sneaking suspicion that he wouldn't have been much better off than he was now. Better for him to work night and day than to work with someone who didn't suit.

His only hope was to talk the locum, should he be lucky enough to find one, into staying indefinitely as he'd claimed he would. If not, well, the viral epidemic sweeping through town this winter had to end some time, didn't it?

You could always ask Dixie.

No, he told himself as he toyed with his pen. Dixie Albright, in spite of being quite attractive with her delicate features, tawny curls, and a mouth that seemed immensely kissable, had one major strike against her. She was Ned's cousin, which, after the stunts he'd pulled, wasn't a favorable recommendation. If he was foolish enough to let her fill in for her cousin, he knew what would come next. She'd turn those beautiful big brown eyes on him and spend the next few weeks convincing him to give Edward Bentley another chance. She'd trowel on the guilt like a heavy-handed mason until she finally gave in.

Well, it wouldn't happen. He'd stand firm. A man had to be accountable for his actions and Mark had already given Ned two chances. That, in itself, was two more than he would have given a year ago.

Why she'd bother taking up her cousin's cause was anyone's guess, although that *was* what people did for their relatives, even the undeserving ones. If he was in trouble, the entire Cameron clan would rally around him, but the difference between him and Ned was that Mark didn't make his own trouble. And if Dixie was familiar enough with Ned's routine to know that he kept a spare house key in his top drawer of his desk, then Mark would lay odds that this wasn't the first time she'd flown to her cousin's rescue.

No, Dixie could pack up Ned's possessions and he would chalk this episode up to experience. If nothing else, he'd learned that disobeying his instincts was a prescription for disaster, which was another reason for refusing her offer.

And yet…she had spunk, he grudgingly admitted as he stared through his southern-exposure window at the scrawny pin oak tree he'd planted last summer. No wilting lily, that was for sure, not to mention a body that oozed pure woman. Her blue sweater wasn't tight by any means, but it hugged her form well enough to reveal the curves underneath. Her long skirt had draped trim hips, and even though he could see the bulkiness of her knee brace, it didn't require much effort to imagine shapely legs and slender ankles.

And miles and miles of soft skin.

In all fairness, if Ned wasn't part of the picture, Mark still wouldn't have hired Dixie because she was too great a distraction. Actually, he was quite surprised to realize that; he'd worked with countless women before and had never seen them as anything more than colleagues.

Dixie, however, was different, and he couldn't explain why. He only sensed that he'd never focus on his work if she was within hailing distance. Crazily enough, he'd spent five minutes in her presence and her light, fresh scent still haunted him. Too much of her could change his goals from building his practice to building a family.

Oh, he didn't have anything *against* getting married. He always thought he would at some point, provided he met the right woman at the right time in his life. Even though his brush with death in last summer's plane crash had made him rethink a lot of things, marriage included, this week was definitely *not* the best time. Trying to provide for the medical needs of three times his usual number of patients didn't allow the time or the energy to think past each day. His top priority was to get his practice back on an even keel, and until that happened everything else in his life would have to wait its turn.

All of which meant that while he might be attracted to Dixie, he wouldn't do anything about it. For one thing, pursuing a woman who, as far as he could tell, wasn't his type was foolhardy at best. He wanted someone who was as driven as he was, who shared his vision of success and would work hard to achieve those goals. If Dixie spent her time rescuing her cousin, then she obviously gave up her own commitments and responsibilities to do so.

"Dr Cameron?"

The familiar voice of his nurse, Miranda Joyner, shook him out of his thoughts. "Yeah, what's up?"

Miranda, a woman who was his mother's age and tended to scold him as if she *were* his mother, stood in the doorway, her normally happy face grim.

"We have a problem."

He shrugged. "What's new?" he asked tiredly.

"I'm serious," she insisted. "Rosy Valesquez is here."

Mrs Valesquez was a Mexican national whose husband was employed at a nearby poultry farm. She was nineteen, pregnant with her first child, and couldn't speak a word of English, which presented a challenge on the best of days. They'd gotten around it before because Ned's nurse knew enough Spanish to give basic instructions. Unfortunately she'd taken advantage of Ned's absence to travel to Arizona with her businessman husband. Without her, they had to find someone else to interpret.

"Did she bring someone to translate?"

"No, but translation is the least of our worries," Miranda said darkly. "She's in labor."

First babies took a while, so he wasn't particularly excited. He'd count himself lucky if she delivered within the next twelve hours. "We'll check her to see how much she's dilated and if she's far enough along, we'll send her to the hospital. What's the word for hospital?"

Miranda shook her gray head. "I don't know and if I did, it's too late. She's crowning."

Crowning? Even if he called an ambulance, she would probably deliver before the crew arrived.

"OK," he said, resigned to turning an exam room into a

delivery suite. "Ask Jane to call for an ambulance and I'll see how much time we have."

Sure enough, Miranda was right. The Valesquez baby would arrive in the next few minutes with or without his help.

Miranda quickly opened an obstetric pack and prepared the field while Mark nodded encouragingly at his patient and promised her that it would soon be over. As he gowned and gloved, he doubted if she understood him, but a soothing tone of voice transcended all language barriers.

"I wonder why she came here instead of heading for the maternity ward?" he mused, fixing his mask in place. "She's been taking Lamaze classes."

"Couldn't tell you. For all we know, she didn't understand her instructor during her childbirth preparation sessions. Or maybe she was just too rattled to remember."

Miranda bustled past him to lay out the few supplies they had available. His office, though well equipped, wasn't designed to handle emergencies of this sort. He didn't have the drugs or equipment if something should go wrong, although it was nice to know the arriving ambulance could help fill in some of the gaps.

Provided it arrived in time.

Mark nudged a stool forward with his shoe, then sat down at the foot of the exam table.

"Don't push," he told Rosy, although he had no idea if she understood him or not. He knew a few Spanish words, but for the life of him he couldn't think of a single one at the moment.

Jane appeared in the doorway. "The ambulance is on the way."

"Did you find someone across the way who could translate?"

His small building stood alone, as did the other buildings that formed the Hope City Medical Complex. While he was the sole occupant of his facility, the others housed two general surgeons, three internists, and two pediatricians. Surely someone within walking distance was bilingual.

"Everyone's still at lunch."

It figured. "In that case, you can be my assistant."

Jane sounded horrified and her face blanched. "Me?"

"Yes, you."

"Sorry, Doctor." She waved her hands for emphasis. "But blood and I don't mix."

"They will today," he said grimly. "Miranda has to look after the baby, so I need you to be my go-fer."

"I have a better idea. I'll get Dr Albright."

"No. You can do it," he insisted. "I'll walk you through everything."

"If I'm on the floor, you won't," she muttered. "I know my limitations and delivering babies is way beyond that."

"If you want my opinion—" Miranda began.

He didn't, but knew he'd hear it regardless.

"It would make more sense to have Dr Albright standing by," Miranda said matter-of-factly. "Do you realize how long it's been since I've assisted in a birth? We can use all the experienced professional help we can get."

"Don't forget, she has a bum knee. Besides, delivering a baby is like riding a bike. It'll come back to you," he said over Rosy's wail and a flurry of Spanish while he concentrated on easing out the baby's head.

"Are you willing to risk it if it doesn't?" she persisted. "We're already working under less than ideal conditions."

He was more aware of that than she realized, but it grated on him to ask for Dixie's help.

"As for her knee," Miranda continued, "why don't you let her decide if she can handle the job? If nothing else, she can serve in an advisory capacity and look over my shoulder."

As much as he wanted to find fault with Miranda's defense of Dixie, he couldn't. If something went wrong... If Ned were here, he wouldn't hesitate to ask for his assistance, so why did he balk at asking Dixie for the same thing?

Before he could send Jane to find the spare doctor in the

house, the soft, lilting voice that would haunt his dreams for weeks to come drifted into the room.

"I heard the commotion. Can you use an extra pair of hands?"

CHAPTER TWO

"EAVESDROPPING?" Mark asked.

Dixie didn't want to admit that while she hadn't been standing outside the door, she *had* been monitoring the situation from a distance. She'd been delighted when the receptionist had tracked her down and saw it as an opportunity to convince him to keep her around. "Jane said you might need some help."

"I didn't know she'd left," he groused.

Uh-oh. Jane had obviously acted without his authorization and she tried to protect the receptionist. "I would have come even if she hadn't asked," Dixie added mildly. "Doctors don't deliver babies in their office every day. Unless, of course, you do things differently here."

"I don't."

Dixie didn't think that he did. He was a by-the-book sort, which was good, but it was also bad because sometimes rules were meant to be broken.

He continued. "Apparently Rosy here didn't understand that she was supposed to go to the hospital when her labor pains were twenty minutes apart."

"Did you call an ambulance?" Dixie asked.

"They're on their way," Jane interjected, back in the room.

"Are you expecting any problems?"

"No," he said. "It should be a routine delivery."

"Then you have everything under control," Dixie commented, aware that her services weren't required or desired. Because she never stayed where she wasn't wanted, even if she was exactly where she wanted to be, she turned toward the door. "I'll leave you all to your fun."

"Wait." He stopped to suction out the baby's mouth and nose before he continued.

"Miranda has decided she's out of her league. If you want to make yourself useful, you can take care of the baby."

The glance he shot the older nurse suggested that he knew she was fully capable of handling whatever medical situation they encountered. She didn't cower under his sharp gaze, but simply shrugged and looked innocent, as if she was so accustomed to his bark that it no longer bothered her.

Inwardly Dixie smiled. Clearly, Mark's staff was staging a mutiny. She'd thank them for their efforts later. Right now, she had a newborn to consider.

"Provided," he continued darkly, "you're up to the physical strain."

"I'll be fine," she answered without hesitation as she propped her crutches in a corner. The room was small enough that she could maneuver quite well without them. As Miranda handed her a towel and showed her the section of counter where she'd set up the basic supplies to care for a newborn, Dixie asked, "What's the situation?"

"You mean, other than the obvious?" He turned to Rosy, although he knew she didn't understand. "Easy now."

When Rosy grunted and bore down once again, he yelled, "No. No. Easy."

The girl let out a spate of Spanish words and Mark released his own frustration. "Where in the hell is a translator when you need one?"

Suddenly realizing the problem, Dixie immediately spoke to the girl in her own language. Mark may have grudgingly accepted her for her medical skills but, whether he realized it or not, she now had an edge.

And she intended to capitalize on it as much as possible.

Although Mark didn't understand what Dixie was saying to his patient, it was obvious that she was quite fluent and well able to get her points across.

At once the girl stopped pushing and started to pant. Her face glistened with sweat and her hair hung damply against her forehead, but even from his position he could see the gratitude in her eyes as she listened to Dixie's instructions.

He delivered the baby's left shoulder, then the right, as he listened to Dixie utter what he thought sounded like words of encouragement.

A few seconds later the entire infant slid into his waiting hands.

"A beautiful little girl," he said as he placed the baby on Rosy's stomach and cut the cord, while Dixie broke the news to their patient. An instant later the separation of mother and infant complete, he handed the newborn over to Dixie, who enfolded the baby in a fluffy white towel and carried her to another corner of the room.

"Where's Jane?" he asked.

"She left again," Miranda answered.

The woman was like a wisp of smoke, he grumbled to himself. Here one minute and gone the next.

"You couldn't tell, but she was looking a little green," Miranda commented. "I didn't think you wanted her on the floor, so I told her she could go back to her phones."

"I wanted her to check on that ambulance."

"I'm sure she is."

While he waited to deliver the placenta, part of him was conscious of the quiet that had descended upon the room when there should have been a baby's cry. A glance at Dixie's corner showed her working on a baby that didn't have the healthy pink skin tones he wanted to see. A deafening silence filled the next few seconds until he couldn't contain himself.

"What's going on over there?" he barked.

"Be patient."

He heard the unmistakable sounds of more suctioning before Dixie's croon. "Come on, sweetheart. You have an impatient mama and a grumpy old doctor who want to hear your voice."

A grumpy old doctor? Was that how she saw him? Grumpy *and* old? How could she say that? At thirty-five, he couldn't be much more than a year or two older than her.

As for being grumpy, that wasn't a big surprise. However, she should know better than to expect him to be all smiles and sunshine when he was run off his feet. If she had ER qualifications, then she'd endured her share of stress too...unless she was the same free-spirited person that her cousin was, which meant that she couldn't be counted on either.

Speaking of which, Mark itched to see for himself what Dixie was doing to their new arrival. What did he truly know about Dixie or her credentials? She may be a physician, but he knew that having "MD" after one's name didn't reflect one's level of competence. If only he could rush this final part of the delivery process, but if he did, his troubles—and Rosy's—would just be starting. The complications of pulling on the cord rather than letting it detach on its own were horrific. He simply had to be patient.

"Talk to me," he demanded of Dixie. "I want a play-by-play narration of what you're doing."

"Don't worry," she said calmly. "We're coming along nicely." After a brief pause, she added, "Are you always this uptight?"

"I'm entitled," he ground out. Instead of talking to him, he heard her speak to the baby. "What's going on over there?" he demanded again.

Suddenly, there was a loud gasp, and the baby answered with an angry cry.

Dixie chuckled. "Our little miss has finally decided to join us. She's pink, has all her fingers and toes, and is gorgeous."

"Apgar?" He wanted to know the score assessing the baby's condition, not how pretty it was. All newborns were red and wrinkly and, in his opinion, quite homely. Beauty, as they said, was in the eye of the beholder.

"Eight. As I said, she's doing fine. She was a little lazy about breathing at first, but she finally got the hang of it."

Rosy rattled off something, but the only word Mark caught was "*bambino*."

Dixie showed the new mother her wrapped bundle and

spoke softly. Mark caught a familiar word here and there but, between his language barrier and looking after Rosy herself, he didn't get much out of their conversation. When Rosy suddenly burst into tears and started wailing, he was glad that Dixie was there. Consoling a weepy woman was hard enough when they both spoke the same language. Consoling one when neither could make themselves understood was next to impossible.

Dixie talked to Rosy for a while and as soon as she wiped the new mother's face with a wet washcloth, Rosy calmed down and smiled through her tears.

"What was all that about?" he asked.

"She's upset about her husband not being here. I told her it was OK, that she'd have time to freshen up and look extra-pretty before he saw her. He can get in on the fun next time."

He didn't doubt for a second that Rosy and her husband would give their daughter brothers and sisters.

"And if he missed the birth of his second child, she could…" She paused and grinned. "Never mind. It's a woman thing. I'd be drummed out of the sisterhood if I said another word."

"Something truly mean and memorable, I suppose."

Her eyes twinkled. "Absolutely."

The door opened and Jane poked her head inside. "Are things presentable in here?"

Miranda had been working to clear away as much evidence of the birth as she could, although it would take a lot of work to restore the room to its pre-delivery-room appearance. "More or less," he answered. "Why?"

"Mr Valesquez is with me."

"Great. Send him in."

Jose Valesquez, a young, attractive man in his early twenties, rushed to his wife's side. Worry was evident on his face and as soon as he grabbed her hand, words flew.

Meanwhile, Mark massaged Rosy's uterus and kept a close eye out for any hemorrhaging. Yet the excitement in their voices was infectious and he couldn't help but steal a glance at the happy couple.

No, they weren't a couple. They were a *family*.

Jose would come home every night to a doting wife and a daughter who'd be delighted to see him. There'd be smiles and giggles and, when his child grew older, tosses in the air and a plea to ''Read me a story, Daddy.'' In Spanish, of course.

Quite the opposite of what went on at his house, where the only greeting was the gurgle of the aquarium that the pet store maintained for him. His fish collection might be awesome to look at and quite gregarious when he sprinkled food in the water, but that sort of welcome didn't compare to a warm human hug.

How strange. The idea had never bothered him before. He must be more tired than he realized. Maybe he was coming down with something…

Dixie passed the baby to the father, then moved next to Mark to peer over his shoulder. ''No tears. I'm impressed.''

''This isn't the first baby I've delivered.''

''I can tell.'' She didn't sound flippant or sarcastic, so he didn't quite know how to take her comment. Instead, he turned the tables.

''I didn't know you spoke Spanish.''

She shrugged. ''You didn't ask.''

''You speak it very well.''

''I get by.''

''Did you take classes?''

''I had a Spanish-speaking roommate in college. Neither of us had extra money, so we worked out a deal where she taught me Spanish and I tutored her in chemistry.''

''You would have paid her for lessons instead of taking a course by yourself?''

''I would have helped her for nothing, but she wouldn't accept it for free. Trading her knowledge for mine helped her save face and I learned something that I wouldn't have otherwise.''

He wondered how many other people would have walked the extra mile like she did in order to salvage someone else's pride. The fact that she did was impressive.

She grinned. "To be honest, her student didn't catch on as fast as mine did."

"It sounds to me like you did."

Once again, she dismissed his praise with a shrug. "What can I say? She was a taskmaster and pride kept me plugging away. The payoff came when I went to med school. I'm at a first-grade level when it comes to reading and writing, but I can hold my own in a conversation. You'd be amazed at how many times being bilingual has helped me in the ER."

"I can imagine," he said as he thought about the difficulties he'd encountered in his own practice.

"As another benefit, her parents owned a restaurant called Poncho's. I ate there more times than I'd care to count. To show their gratitude for helping Luisa pass her course, they also shared a few of their recipes. I can make the absolute best enchiladas and salsa you'll ever eat."

Ironically enough, he wondered if he'd ever have the opportunity to taste them. Spicy Mexican food was his weakness.

"Do you have a large number of obstetric patients?" she asked.

He was almost sorry to change the subject. He didn't want to get to know her, but admittedly these bits and pieces were interesting.

"A fair amount," he replied. "We're working to bring in an OB-GYN, so if that comes about, I'm sure all of the family practitioners will see fewer obstetric cases. As for me, even if my numbers don't decrease, it will be great to have someone local to handle any problems. Speaking of which, how's your knee holding up?"

"To be honest, between my pain pill and the excitement, I'd forgotten all about it," she confessed. "I guess that means I'm well on the road to recovery."

"Don't overdo things," he warned gruffly as he cast a side-long glance at her.

"I won't."

For the next few minutes he concentrated on finishing up his duties with Rosy. Baby Valesquez was still in her dad's arms and, to judge from the lack of noise coming from her, either perfectly content or fast asleep. Mother and father were speaking quietly and Dixie…

Dixie was standing off to one side, gazing at the young family with the most longing expression he'd ever seen. Had her biological clock started ticking?

More importantly, did she have a significant other in her life?

Irritated that the question had crossed his mind, he focused on his patient. "Did you ever find out why she came here instead of the hospital? Didn't she realize she was in the final stage of labor?"

"She was waiting for her husband to come back after he finished an out-of-town job he'd taken on the side to supplement their income. Her labor pains weren't regular, so she didn't worry until they suddenly started coming five minutes apart. She knew she was supposed to come here first to be checked, so she did."

"And by then she was too late."

"Exactly." Dixie's attention remained riveted on the couple. "What a perfect picture. That baby has already wrapped her daddy's heart around her little finger."

He glanced at the new family. "Sure. It's a father-daughter thing."

Dixie chuckled. "Genetically ingrained, I suppose."

"So my sisters tell me. By the way, I heard you talking to the baby in Spanish when you were working on her. What did you say?"

"Oh, I just told her that she'd miss out on a lot of fun things like dances and proms if she checked out now." She giggled. "It must have worked because she started breathing on her own."

Jane returned at that moment, a step ahead of the ambulance crew, which consisted of two familiar faces, paramedic Annie McCall Tremaine and her EMT partner, Mic Haines.

"Giving the maternity ward some competition?" Annie teased as she and Mic wheeled in the gurney.

Mark laughed. "Just trying to keep my office staff on their toes. They're lucky I was here, otherwise they might have had to handle this on their own."

He was conscious of Annie glancing at Dixie. "Looks like you had plenty of help."

"This is Dr Albright. Dixie, Annie. And Mic." Under the circumstances, he thought it best not to advertise Dixie's relationship to Ned. With Ned gone and Dixie leaving in a few days, it seemed pointless to give a lengthy introduction. And if Annie *should* ask, he'd simply announce that she was a locum.

Annie smiled. "Pleased to meet you."

"Same here," Dixie murmured.

Annie eyed the mother. "Anything we should know about?"

"A routine delivery. Baby's Apgar was eight after delivery." He turned to Dixie. "Can you tell Rosy and her husband that they'll take her to the hospital just as a precaution for both her and the baby? If all goes well, they can go home tomorrow."

Dixie obliged. Within a few minutes Rosy and daughter were on their way to the ambulance while Jose pumped Mark's hand and rattled off a string of Spanish.

"He's thanking you for looking after his wife," she murmured.

"I guessed that," he said. "Tell him I'll stop in at the hospital later this evening to check on Rosy and the baby."

She did, and as soon as Jose hurried out of the room she hesitated, as if she hated to leave. Mark assumed that after the afternoon's drama, sorting through Ned's desk was as appealing as the prospect of a colonoscopy.

"I should get back to Ned's office."

For his peace of mind, she definitely should. "Thanks for stepping in," he said instead.

"You're welcome." With that, she tucked her crutches under one arm and left the room.

To Mark's surprise, the bright, upbeat atmosphere suddenly changed to a bleakness that matched the winter landscape. He didn't know how Dixie had managed it, but she had taken all the warmth in the room with her.

Dixie parked in her cousin's driveway and stared at his house gratefully. In comparison to her bungalow, it was a large building with a wide porch, and obviously built within the last ten years, but, regardless of its newness, it represented a haven that at the moment she needed desperately.

In the next breath, though, her relief sprouted into worry as she noted the yards of ice-covered concrete that stretched between her and the front door. Idly, she wondered what her doctor would say if he knew what she was going to do. He may have given his permission to drive—she didn't have to use her left leg to operate a gas pedal or a clutch—but she doubted if it included navigating icy paths on foot.

You can do this, she told herself as she turned up her parka's collar to protect her ears from the cold. *The sidewalk probably isn't as slick as it looks.*

She eyed the distance and fought her fear of falling. If something happened, she had her cellphone and could call for help. Consoling herself with that thought, she braced herself against the cold, opened the door and somehow managed to drag her crutches out with her.

Not certain if she could make this trip again, she slung her purse and the sack of papers she'd gathered from Ned's office over her left shoulder.

With cautious steps, she skirted her little Pontiac and headed toward the porch. Each advance required a carefully orchestrated balancing act and intense concentration because the going was as treacherous as she'd feared. When a crutch slipped in one spot and nearly sent her tumbling, she froze and willed her pounding heart to slow down.

"You'll make it," she encouraged herself aloud between deep breaths. "You're halfway there."

In fact, if she hadn't gotten that far, she would have turned back and driven to a hotel. It didn't seem worth the risk to her knee to continue, and yet what choice did she have?

Unfortunately, at the rate she was going, she'd freeze into a Popsicle before she even got to the front door. Her exertion had warmed her inside and out, but just standing still for these few minutes was enough to cool her down.

Before she could will herself to move again, she heard her name yelled across the yard. Relieved that she wasn't alone, she gratefully glanced at the newcomer. Her welcoming smile turned to a gasp of surprise as Mark walked toward her with the surefootedness of a mountain goat.

He was definitely a sight for sore eyes. Although his head was uncovered, he wore black leather gloves, a black trench coat that hung to his knees, and a gray scarf around his neck.

"Wait for me," he called out.

"Like I'm going anywhere," she mumbled. Although he was the last person she would have expected to be her savior, she wouldn't refuse his offer of help. The big question in her mind was why he'd bothered to drop by. He hadn't spoken to her all afternoon and she'd received the distinct impression that she couldn't leave soon enough to suit him.

"This is a surprise," she quipped.

"It wouldn't be if you hadn't slunk out of the office without a word."

"Excuse me," she sputtered. "I didn't know I was expected to check in and out with you."

"You aren't." He sounded gruff. "I just wanted to make sure you wouldn't be doing what you're doing now."

She stared at him, incredulous. "I'm going to my cousin's house."

"And not doing too well at it either, I might add."

She drew herself up to her full five and a half feet. "I may not be running any races or setting any records, but I'm doing just fine.''

He pointedly glanced at the distance remaining. ''How long did it take you to get this far?''

Too long, but she wouldn't admit it. ''I'm not timing myself.''

His mouth twitched as if he'd read her thoughts. ''You have no business navigating outdoors by yourself. It's too dangerous, which is why you should have told someone you were on your way here. Good grief, woman, the house has been empty for days, we had an ice storm a few days ago and no one's cleared the walk. You're an accident waiting to happen.''

For a woman who'd been independent for years and was the problem-fixer in the family, it was quite novel to be on the receiving end of someone's concern. ''I can't help it. Everyone was busy, including you.''

''You could have stopped me.''

''When? You whizzed in and out of exam rooms all afternoon. If I heard your voice in the hallway and thought I could catch you, you'd disappeared by the time I got there myself.''

A wry smile tugged at his mouth. ''We were a little busy today.''

''I'll say. For a few minutes, I almost thought I was back in the ER on a Saturday night.''

''Which is where you might have landed if I hadn't driven by and seen you.''

''Why, Dr Cameron...'' she batted her eyelashes at him ''...I didn't know you cared.''

He locked his fingers around her elbow. ''You helped me and I'm returning the favor.''

''Really?'' She didn't know quite what to think. He didn't seem the type to worry about returning favors.

''I'm also trying to give myself an evening off, which I won't if I have to go to the ER because you hurt yourself.''

She wondered why he thought she'd call him if she had a

problem, then decided to let it slide. "Don't you have regular ER physicians?"

"We do, but if they get busy, we take turns with back-up. And sometimes, if one of our patients has a major problem, like an acute MI, or needs surgery, the ER doc contacts us."

"And you come running."

"Yes." He stared down at her. "I don't know about you, but it's too cold to be standing outside visiting."

"Yeah, my nose is frozen." So was everything else.

And yet warmth had started to build inside her—a warmth that she directly attributed to Mark's hand on her arm and the knowledge that for all his bluster he wasn't as cold-hearted as he'd first appeared.

If Ned had been within grabbing distance, she would have shaken him for causing this man so much grief.

"Nose, ears, feet," he agreed. "And parts in between."

His nose and ears were pink from the near-zero temperature, but the rest of him appeared perfectly fine. Heat emanated from his body and she was extremely glad that nature had built him large enough to block most of the north wind.

"I hate to mention this…" she began.

"Mention what?"

"Can you get my suitcase from the trunk?"

He held out his hand. "Keys?"

She dug in her coat pocket and placed the keyring in his palm. While he returned to her car, she started to take another step toward the house, but he obviously had eyes in the back of his head because he issued a terse warning.

"Don't move until I get back."

"But—"

"But nothing." He turned to meet her gaze. "You can either wait or forget the suitcase. Your choice."

"Dictator."

"So I've been told." He raised an eyebrow.

"I'll wait," she acquiesced.

With an agility and speed that she envied, he retrieved her

case and hauled it to the porch. "What did you pack in here?" he asked. "This weighs a ton."

"It does not," she protested mildly.

"Does, too. How long were you planning to stay?"

"A few weeks. Less if Ned comes back before then."

"*If* Ned comes back at all." He returned to take her arm once again.

"He will." He had to. Imagining the scene if she had to deliver *that* depressing news to her aunt, she shuddered.

"I know you're cold, but we won't be out here much longer."

Mark had obviously misinterpreted the reason for her shiver, but it would take too long to enlighten him. "I'm OK."

"Then let's go."

He held onto her arm as she carefully swung herself forward on her crutches. The worn rubber feet slipped on the ice and if it hadn't been for Mark's strong hold, she would easily have landed on her backside.

He paused. "This isn't working. Give me those."

"Give you what? My crutches?"

"Yes." He took them and propped them against the porch railing. "We're going to do this instead."

Without warning, he hauled her close to him until she was plastered against his side and held in position with one strong arm around her waist.

He was so warm and so solid—a veritable rock of steadiness and stability.

Tucked under his arm, the faint scent of his aftershave was enough to send her hormones into overdrive. It was fresh and clean and carried a hint of spice that mingled with the woodsy outdoor aroma of someone's fireplace.

Whoever snagged this man would be one lucky woman.

"Ready?" he asked.

No, she wanted to say. "Yes."

"Then here goes. Just relax and let me do all the work."

It was like having her legs back again. She hadn't moved

this fast since before her mishap with a patch of snow-covered ice. He half carried her along the sidewalk and the only thing she had to do was hang on.

With her arm around his waist, it certainly wasn't a hardship. He was lean and hard and fit against her, as if their bodies were designed to be that way. Idly, she couldn't think of a nicer Valentine's gift than to see him in swim trunks.

"Were you a Boy Scout?" she asked impulsively.

"No, why?"

"Because I feel like I'm one of those little old ladies that Boy Scouts escort across busy streets."

He laughed, and she was close enough to feel it reverberate in his chest.

"Believe me, you're not anywhere close to being a little old lady."

She grinned at him. "I'm glad you think so."

He stopped at the steps. "Hold on."

She hadn't let go—didn't *want* to let go—but she nodded anyway. Inch-thick ice coated the steps, but he managed to take them without any problem.

Although the ice on the porch itself was less thick because the roof had given it some protection from the elements, he held onto her even after they'd reached the door.

"Can you stand on your own?" he asked.

"I think so." She hated to give up her anchor, but she couldn't hang onto him for ever. He, too, seemed reluctant to step away, which made her wonder about his reasons... Was he that worried she couldn't stand on her own two feet, or did he feel the same connection, the same flash of electricity, that she did?

"I'll get your crutches," he said, still glued to her side.

For an instant, the idea of a kiss floated through her brain. The only thing needed to make it happen would be to stand on tiptoe.

The expression in his eyes suggested that the thought had occurred to him, too. Something hot, something primal appeared on his face before the moment passed as quickly as it had arrived.

Disconcerted by her own attack of sudden desire for a man who clearly was the least likely candidate she could have chosen, she dropped her arm and stepped back. This time she was grateful for the cold air because she could think of no better way to cool her overheated face.

Telling herself to forget about the incident and chalk up her response to some strange shift in barometric pressure, she once again dug in her coat pocket and removed Ned's spare key. The door opened easily and she hobbled inside while Mark flicked on the light switch and set her case on the entryway floor.

The closed-in smell greeted her, but so did the central heating, which had been Dixie's main concern. If the household utilities hadn't been working, she would have faced the unwelcome possibility of a return trek to her car.

With Mark beside her, the idea of walking back to her vehicle didn't seem like a horrifying prospect at all.

Her other concern had been the overall condition of Ned's house. Her cousin wasn't particularly neat on a good day, and because he'd disappeared on such short notice she could hardly imagine how much penicillin might be growing in his kitchen.

"This sounds crazy," she began, "but I almost feel like I'm intruding."

"He'd let you stay here if he knew you were coming, wouldn't he?" he asked practically.

"Yes, but that's the problem. He *isn't* here to give permission."

"If it bothers you that much, you can always go to a hotel. Or go home."

She dismissed his hotel suggestion. She'd been too frugal all her life to spend money when it wasn't necessary. As for going home, she'd come to do what she could to locate Ned. Until she accomplished her mission, she was staying right where she was.

"I'll be fine," she commented.

"Are you afraid of what you'll find?"

Startled by his uncanny assessment, Dixie met his gaze with wide eyes. "Do you know that you have the most remarkable ability to read minds?"

He shrugged and another small grin tugged at his mouth. If he ever deigned to bestow a full, genuine smile on her, he'd be absolutely breathtaking. "It's a gift," he teased.

Knowing she couldn't postpone the inevitable, Dixie took a bracing breath. Mark would probably never know how glad she was that she wasn't alone on her first walk-through of Ned's home.

"You realize that he's not here," he said kindly.

However illogical, the possibility of finding his body had crossed her mind. "I know. I'm just being silly."

"Not really. If it will make you feel better, I'll walk through every room before I leave."

She squared her shoulders, determined not to show any more signs of weakness to the man who clearly disdained all such signs. "Thanks for offering. I'll think about it."

She maneuvered herself through the short entryway and entered the living room. There, she stood and stared in amazement at the sight before her.

"My word!" she exclaimed, hardly able to believe her own eyes. "What happened here?"

CHAPTER THREE

MARK glanced around the room. As far as he could tell, it appeared like most living rooms in the country, including his. Other than a big-screen television set, which he envied, the usual sofa, recliner, a floor lamp and a coffee-table with medical journals stacked on top took up nearly all the space.

"What's wrong?" he asked. "Everything looks fine to me."

Dixie ambled forward on her crutches. "That's just it. It looks fine. It shouldn't."

He frowned. "You *want* the place to be trashed?"

"Not trashed," she corrected. "Lived in."

Once again, Mark took stock of his surroundings. Adventure paperbacks, medical magazines, several framed photos, the TV guide, and a pair of oversized stuffed pandas—the sort carnival-goers won—were the same things he'd seen the last time he'd been inside Ned's house.

"It doesn't look any different than when Ned hosted a pre-hospital Christmas party here during the holidays," he said. "Of course, the Christmas tree is gone, but it looks to me like Ned lives here."

She rolled her eyes as if his powers of observation were suspect. "I said 'lived in' not 'lived.' It's too clean and neat."

"Some men do know how to pick up after themselves," he reminded her.

"Some men, yes. Not Ned," she insisted. "He doesn't stack his magazines or papers neatly. They're usually scattered all over the place. Instead of washing his coffee-cups, he dirties another until he's used every one and *has* to wash them. His books are normally shoved every which way in the bookcase. And…" she leaned over to swipe the coffee-table's

38

surface with a gloved finger "…he wouldn't know which end of a duster to use if his life depended on it."

She held up her finger to display the lack of surface dust. "If he disappeared ten days ago, I would have expected to see a little dirt around here. His office certainly had plenty of it."

"Our cleaning service has strict orders to only vacuum the floors," he said stiffly. "Our desks are sacred unless otherwise specified."

"I'm not faulting your maintenance crew or your standards. I'm simply pointing out that this…" she waved her arms "…is out of character for Ned. It's also out of the ordinary for a man who supposedly hasn't set foot in this house for over a week."

"Are you saying that Ned hasn't disappeared?"

"I'm not saying anything. I'm only making observations." She picked up an envelope on the top of the neatly stacked pile on the coffee-table. "Here's something else that's odd. This is postmarked with yesterday's date. Unless your postmen give more personal service than they provide in other cities, these letters should still be lying on the floor in the entryway near the letter slot."

She headed toward the door.

"Where are you going?" he asked.

"To the kitchen."

Mark followed her there and watched her go directly to the refrigerator. As far as he could tell from peering over her shoulder, the only things inside were the usual bottles of condiments, an unopened bottle of sparkling grape juice, and a jar of green olives.

She exchanged a worried glance with him. "See?"

"See what? It's obvious that he's not hiding out in his own house if the refrigerator is empty."

"True, but his note said he was leaving town for a three-day weekend, right?"

"Yeah, so?"

She fell silent, as if trying to fit these pieces together into a recognizable picture. "Then, a week later, he called to say he'd run into problems and would be gone for a while longer."

"More or less."

"Don't you get it?" she said, her face alight with excitement. "You don't clean out your refrigerator if you're only going to be away from home for a few days. Which means that someone had to come in afterwards and take care of these little details."

"Unless he knew ahead of time that he wasn't coming back."

She shook her head. "Ned doesn't plan that far ahead."

Mark disagreed, but decided to let it slide for reasons of his own. "Maybe he didn't plan to be more than three days, but his refrigerator could be empty because he didn't have anything in there to start with," he pointed out. "My fridge doesn't look much better than his and I haven't left town."

"Maybe not, but Ned loves milk. Chocolate milk. He always has a carton on hand. Now, though, he doesn't."

"He could have drunk it before he left and didn't bother buying a replacement."

She pointed to the waste bin near the door leading to the garage. "Then why is the trash empty? There isn't as much as a used envelope in there."

"He emptied the trash can before he left."

She shook her head. "You don't understand. Ned doesn't worry about little details like that. Someone has been here recently—and I'm not talking about us."

"Then he obviously has a housekeeping service who came some time during the past couple of days. For all we know, he called them after he called me, told them he'd be gone indefinitely and asked if they would clean out his refrigerator."

A wrinkle appeared on her forehead. "It's possible," she grudgingly agreed, "but Ned has never hired a cleaning lady in his entire life. He simply doesn't consider mundane things like that, much less worry about coming home to sour milk or soggy lettuce.''

"Maybe he's changed." Listening to himself, he could hardly believe he'd just defended his colleague. To be honest, up until these past two weeks he would have agreed that Ned flew by the seat of his pants and didn't concern himself with such petty things as neatness and spoiled groceries. But now…he wasn't so sure. Yet he hated to see Dixie so upset when, in Mark's opinion, Ned wasn't worth her concern.

"Let's say he didn't call anyone else," he went on. "The cleaning service might have been conscientious enough to throw out his perishables without being asked."

"The point is, he might have talked to someone in town besides you. He or she might know where he is."

The excitement in her eyes was blinding. He hated to be the one to dash her hopes but, as far as he could tell, she was setting herself up for a major disappointment. "By the time you track down whoever that might be, Ned will have decided to come back on his own."

She pressed her mouth into a line and he had a sudden urge to kiss it back into its usual smile. Finally, her shoulders slumped ever so slightly. "You're right. I still want to know where he is, though. I just couldn't live with myself if I assumed that he was *able* to return whenever he wanted, and found out later that he was in a situation where he *couldn't*."

"Don't let your imagination run wild," he advised. "He's obviously not injured, or he wouldn't have been so secretive when he called." Unless he'd been in jail, and if that was the case…

"As difficult as it is," he added, "you have to accept his choices and live with them."

"Part of me says I should wait him out, but I can't," she said ruefully. "Old habits die hard. You see, his parents—my aunt and uncle—took me in when I was ten. Being the oldest, I was supposed to keep an eye on Ned. I always did."

"And you still are."

She nodded. "My Aunt Cora is frantic. She can't believe he wouldn't call and tell her his plans. He always has before."

"He may have gotten mixed up in something he shouldn't have." Considering the shady circumstances of Ned's disappearance, Mark's theory was just as plausible as any other.

She sighed. "That's what I'm afraid of, which is why I came. If Ned is in trouble, I have to do something. For my aunt's sake."

He understood completely. Minimizing a loved one's pain was something one did. Sadly, Ned needed a strong dose of tough love from his family. It was apparent that they wouldn't give him what he needed or deserved, but Mark certainly didn't have any qualms about forcing Ned to pay the proverbial piper. If Ned weren't hip-deep in problems wherever he was, he would be when he got back.

Mark intended to ask for details about her game plan, but stopped as soon as he noticed the dark circles under her eyes. Dixie was clearly exhausted from a day that had been stressful enough to sap the energy from a healthy person, much less someone who'd recently had knee surgery.

"Whatever you do can wait," he told her as he pulled out a kitchen chair. "Sit down before you fall down. I'll make some coffee as soon as I turn up the thermostat."

"I won't fall down," she said indignantly, but Mark noticed that she obeyed.

"If you say so." He found the thermostat in the living room, adjusted the temperature upwards and then rejoined her in the kitchen.

Fortunately, the coffee-maker and a canister of grounds stood in full view on the counter. Before long, he set a steaming cup of coffee in front of her. "Sugar?"

"No. And I like it black."

"Good," he said as he sat across from her. "Because I have no idea where the sugar is and we both know there isn't a drop of milk in the house."

She'd slipped her coat off and closed her eyes as she sipped the hot drink. "Perfect," she said as she licked her lips. "Is this another one of your many talents?"

He forced his gaze off her mouth, wondering how she could turn such an instinctive move into something so provocative.

"Necessity is the mother of invention. If I want coffee, I have to make it myself."

"Jane doesn't keep the pot filled?"

He grimaced. "Not if I can help it. Her coffee tastes like dishwater."

"Hmm." She grinned. "I've never tasted that."

"Neither have I, but after drinking Jane's brew I have a good idea."

"What about Miranda?"

"Miranda is another story. She made it plain that coffee-making isn't in her job description, which is OK because I need a top-notch nurse more than anything."

"Has she always worked for you?"

"I inherited her from Dr Richmond. She rules the roost, so to speak."

"And you let her."

"More or less," he said wryly. "Most of the time she has a strong grasp of what will and won't work in terms of office procedures. To give her credit, she is willing to stay up to date. I've just learned not to fight her on the little things."

"And on the big things?"

"We've learned to compromise."

Her smile reminded him of spring sunshine. "They say that behind every great man stands a woman."

"Whatever you do, don't remind her, although, to be honest, she's a huge asset. If I need something done, no matter how simple or difficult, she's the one to ask. She's great at greasing bureaucratic wheels."

"You're lucky. Sometimes it's not *what* you know, but *who* you know."

"Exactly. I hear that the office girls in the County Clerk's office run when she comes in. She's had the best luck when it comes to appealing her property tax valuations. Personally, I think everyone's afraid of her.''

"Really? She seems so sweet."

"She is," he said, "but she grew up in Hope and knows all the skeletons in people's closets, especially the folks in City Hall."

"How convenient."

"Definitely. But here's a word to the wise…organizations fight to have her on their fund drive campaigns. She single-handedly brought in the most donations last year for the Cancer Society."

"I'll keep my checkbook under lock and key," she promised.

"Good idea."

"Speaking of growing up, are you a Hope native?"

He shook his head. "I'm a transplant, along with about half of the town. I moved here three years ago after I finished my residency."

"And your family?"

"Scattered across the country. Along with a set of parents, there are four of us. Two boys and two girls, although my sister Alison and I are twins."

"A built-in playmate. How nice. It must be wonderful to have a large family."

"It has its moments, but I can't imagine not having a single one of them around."

"You're very fortunate. Ned and I had different enough interests that as we grew older we drifted apart."

"You're both doctors. I'd say that was a similar interest."

"He was the athlete and I wasn't. I had to study for my grades and he didn't. He was brilliant when it came to competitive speech and debate and I was woefully tongue-tied at public speaking of any kind. He won awards for anything and everything and I didn't."

And yet, Mark thought as he leaned back to nurse the rest of his drink, she'd been given the responsibility of looking after Ned—a responsibility that she still shouldered without hesitation. She was clearly loyal to a fault.

And if loyalty was her fault, it was the only one he could see. She might claim not to be athletic, but she certainly had an athlete's form. He knew, because he'd noticed a great deal when he'd half carried her up the sidewalk.

Now, that had been an experience he wouldn't mind repeating. Next time, though, he'd like to do it without the barrier of heavy coats. She'd fitted against him as if she were his other half and if the weather hadn't been so dratted cold, he would have kissed her at the top of the steps until the heat they'd generated melted the ice under their feet.

As it was, he'd hardly been able to take his hands off her once he'd touched her. He'd only managed because he'd remembered his reasons for being there in the first place. Her safety had been on his mind, of course, but his motive went beyond that.

Just tell her why you're here and get it over with.

He should, he knew, but it was rather nice to imagine she was simply a new acquaintance who'd attracted him, rather than a potential answer to a problem. He wasn't quite ready to let that fantasy disappear. It would soon enough.

Sitting at the table in the home of this gorgeous woman, he tried to recall the last time he'd been on an official date. As luck would have it, he'd been on call on the nights when everyone had hosted their Christmas and New Year's Eve parties, so he'd attended alone and had mingled with couples so that his single state hadn't appeared quite so obvious.

"I'm surprised you didn't visit Ned over the holidays," he commented.

"I was on duty." She shrugged. "It seemed more important to let the people with families have time off."

He finished off his coffee, knowing that he probably should go, even though he hated their time together to end. A hundred things were waiting for his attention at home but, strangely enough, he couldn't think of a single one on his list. He was too caught up with watching Dixie's skin color return to its healthy glow after being out in the cold, noticing her graceful—and ringless—hands, and wishing that he could taste the coffee on her lips.

He wondered what she'd do if he leaned across the table and succumbed to his impulse.

She'd think he was crazy, he thought. And yet he could have sworn when they'd been standing on the porch that she would have welcomed his attentions.

Yes, he wanted to kiss her, and more, but he simply had to play it safe for now. Acting impulsively always caused him grief. He hated to think of the number of times he'd met a woman who'd seemed to understand him, only to discover that she had a hidden agenda. Since then he'd vowed to wait for a partner who was interested in Mark Cameron the man, rather than Mark Cameron the doctor.

As for Dixie's agenda, he didn't have to wait to discover what it was. She'd made it plain that she wanted him to give her cousin a second chance, which, short of evidence that he was working as an undercover operative for a government agency, wouldn't happen. By the same token, it would be interesting to see just how far she'd go to ensure that Ned wouldn't lose his job.

Was that why she'd seemed so eager to kiss him?

Was he doing the right thing by coming here, hat in hand, asking for her help?

Miranda had seemed to think so, but now, considering what might have happened if he hadn't practiced self-control, he'd harvested an entire crop of new doubts.

His watch beeped the hour and he glanced at the time. He could hardly believe that sixty minutes had passed so quickly, but he'd never been more grateful for an interruption than now. Dixie presented too great a temptation, and until he got to know her better he'd be a fool to act rashly.

"I'd better go," he said, rising and carrying his mug to the sink. "I still need to drop in at the hospital to check on Mrs Valesquez and her baby."

Dixie grabbed one of the crutches she'd propped against

the table and stood. Although her expression was a little puzzled by his brusque tone, she didn't press him to stay.

"Thanks for everything. I appreciate all your help."

"Before I go, where do you want your suitcase?"

"I can manage."

"Probably," he agreed, although he doubted it. "But why bother if you don't have to?"

She brushed a curly lock off her forehead and he wondered if her tawny hair felt as soft as it looked. "Fine. If you can carry it to the spare bedroom?"

"No problem."

He retrieved her case and followed her to the room in question. As he swung the battered piece of luggage onto the bed, one of the latches popped open and a pile of filmy fabric in an array of bright colors that ranged from dusky rose to red spilled onto the floor.

"Damn," she muttered.

He bent down to pick up the scraps of lace and realized that chivalry might be dead but he obviously wasn't. Handling silk panties that smelled of her fragrance wasn't a wise thing for him to do when he was already trying to maintain his emotional distance.

He tossed the offending articles onto the bed and convinced himself that seeing Dixie's lingerie wasn't any different than seeing his sisters' hanging from the rod in his bathroom. As for Dixie, he was a doctor, for Pete's sake. There wasn't anything regarding the female body that he hadn't seen.

Yet as she leaned over the bed and he caught a glimpse of delicious curves he realized that his medical objectivity had taken a vacation where Dixie was concerned.

It was far too easy to wonder what color she was wearing next to her skin.

Worse yet, he wondered what color she'd choose to wear tomorrow.

He scooped up the rest of the intimate apparel and tried not to notice how soft and silky and sheer the articles were. "I'm going to look for a garage door opener while you take care of…your unpacking.''

Hurrying down the hall, he forced his mind on where Ned might have stashed his spare electronic opener. Considering Dixie's knee surgery, it would be so much easier if she parked her car in the garage until this cold snap passed. She could step out of her car, walk into the house and bypass the icy steps completely.

He started in the laundry room and checked the drawers and cupboards near the washer and dryer. No luck. By the time he came into the kitchen, Dixie was rummaging through the drawers there.

''Maybe he doesn't have a spare,'' she said after they'd hunted through every logical place.

''I'll bet he does. We're just not looking in the right spot.''

''Where else can it be?''

''I don't know, but we'll get around it,'' he said decisively. ''I know a guy who installs automatic openers. He'll program a new control box for you.''

''Ned might not like it,'' she warned.

''He isn't here to complain, is he?''

''I guess not.''

''In the meantime, I'll move your car inside.'' Without giving her time to protest, he found his coat, went into the garage via the door through the kitchen, and raised the garage doors manually. A few minutes later, he drove her car inside.

''Thanks so much,'' she said as he rejoined her. ''You really don't need to go to all this trouble.''

''It's no trouble.''

''I know this is a small way to repay you, but Ned has a huge supply of frozen dinners. Would you like one before you leave?''

''Your famous enchiladas sound better.''

''They do, don't they?''

''I'll have to take a rain-check for now, if that's OK with you.'' He shouldn't, but nothing said he couldn't spend a few pleasant hours with a colleague.

"I'll plan on later in the week, then. Thursday?"

"Thursday it is. As for you, you need to make tonight an early one."

She shrugged, as if she didn't consider his advice important enough to take. "I have a lot to do before I can crawl into bed."

She would have to mention that particular three-letter word. "I'm serious," he insisted. "You won't be much of a help to me tomorrow if you're dead on your feet."

She blinked, clearly taken aback by his announcement. "Excuse me?"

He clearly hadn't led her to this moment very well. Instead, he'd simply blurted out his plan. "I'm accepting your offer to work for me."

She stared at him in obvious surprise. "Are you serious?"

"Sure. I'll pick you up at eight o'clock, sharp."

She shook her head. "Wait a minute. I'm missing something."

"What's to miss? I need another physician and you volunteered. If your credentials check out tomorrow morning, you're my new temporary partner."

A knowing gleam appeared in her eyes. "Your locum canceled, didn't he?"

He hated to admit she was right, but if he didn't she'd see right through his excuses. "Yes."

"I can't stay more than a month," she warned. "That's all the sick time I've requested."

"A month should be adequate. I may not need you that long."

"And Ned's job? Will you hold it open for him?"

"No," he said firmly. "You're here until I can hire a locum or a permanent replacement. Period. Ned is on his own."

"I see." She glanced at the floor as she chewed on her upper lip. After a second's hesitation, she met his gaze. "If you haven't changed your mind about that, why did you change your mind about me working for you?"

"Because I'm desperate," he said bluntly, determined to

stop her from getting the wrong idea. "As Miranda also pointed out, I'd be a fool to let someone qualified slip through my fingers."

"I see."

She glanced away and Mark was afraid that she saw more than he would like.

"She threatened you, didn't she?"

Dixie clearly understood Miranda's role in their office far better than he'd thought she did. Hating to hit her full blast with the truth, he hedged. "Sort of."

"Was she going to quit?"

"So she said." Mark knew that his nurse didn't need a job. She was close to retirement age and her husband had provided well for her when he'd died. Miranda worked because she liked her position in the office and it gave her a reason to get up every morning. He knew the day would come when she'd decide to slow down, but he didn't want that to happen while he was down two physicians. On top of everything else, breaking in a new nurse and teaching her all the ins and outs of Miranda's duties was too horrible to imagine. Working with Dixie seemed the lesser of the two evils.

"I'm surprised you let her win this one."

"It was a mutual decision."

"Well, thanks for the offer but, no, thanks. I don't work where I'm not wanted." She met his gaze without wavering.

"Suit yourself, but you'll have better luck with your search for your cousin if you have access to his office."

Her eyes narrowed. "Meaning I won't otherwise?"

He played a card that she couldn't beat. "Patient confidentiality issues. You understand, don't you?"

"Absolutely," she snapped. "In that case, I accept."

"Good." He turned to leave. "Before I forget, I do have a few conditions."

"Which are?"

"What happens with Ned's job is between him and me. You aren't our mediator, neither are you his defense attorney."

She hesitated. "OK. Anything else?"

"I'll expect complete and total honesty from you."

She appeared affronted. "Of course."

"Your loyalty is to me. If you discover anything about Ned—anything at all, good or bad—I want to know."

"No secrets. Agreed."

"Then I'll see you at eight a.m." He dug in his shirt pocket and pulled out a pen and a scrap of paper. "Here's my home number and my pager number."

She placed his note on the table. "Thanks."

He headed to the door leading into the garage so he could avoid the deathtrap porch steps. "Enjoy what's left of your evening."

"I will."

"Close the garage door behind me," he ordered.

"I will," she repeated. "Goodnight."

Acknowledging her comment with a wave, he hurried outside to his vehicle. He couldn't believe he'd actually gone and hired Dixie Albright. Miranda might think her presence was the perfect solution, but he foresaw nothing but problems.

Dixie was simply too attractive for her own good and for his peace of mind. Although he'd gotten her to agree to his conditions about her cousin, it remained to be seen if she honored them.

If she didn't, she'd be history, he consoled himself as he slid behind the wheel. However, that reassurance didn't quite answer the question burning in his mind.

Had he simply exchanged one disaster for another?

CHAPTER FOUR

"YOU have to do something, Doctor," Carrie Jamison begged as she placed her lethargic six-month-old son on the exam table. "He can hardly breathe."

Dixie watched the infant's chest rise and fall in short gasps as if he couldn't catch his breath. Even without her stethoscope, he sounded wheezy, and every now and again he coughed pitifully. He was far too pale to suit her and she would have liked a pulse oximeter to test his oxygen saturation levels, but she wasn't in the ER with all the high-tech equipment she normally had at her disposal.

"Is he eating?"

"No. He won't take his bottle. At first I thought he just had the usual cold, with his stuffy nose and low-grade fever, but he's getting worse. He pulls on his ears, too."

Dixie warmed her stethoscope between her hands before she placed the flat surface on his chest and listened. "Joey has pneumonia," she told his mother, before she peered into his ears. "To treat him properly, I'm going to run a few tests so I know what we're dealing with."

"I've heard that RSV is going around. Is that what he has?"

"It's possible," Dixie admitted. "Respiratory syncytial virus is prevalent this time of year and our little people are getting hit hard. But whether his test is positive or not, Joey needs to be in the hospital where he can receive regular breathing treatments and IV fluids. How long did you say it's been since he's eaten?"

"A little over twenty-four hours. Are you sure, though, you can't just give him an antibiotic? I'll watch him really close at home."

"He's dehydrated and we have to get fluids in him right away," she told Carrie kindly. "If he was taking his bottle, I'd be willing to try your idea, but he's not. The hospital is the best place for him."

"I can't pay for him to stay there," she said flatly. "My husband changed jobs and our new health insurance isn't effective until the end of the month."

"Joey can't wait until then. You're not the only one in these circumstances," Dixie reassured her. "The hospital will work with you and I know there are charitable programs that can help, too. So don't let finances stop you from giving Joey the care he needs."

Carrie managed a tremulous smile. "OK."

"As soon as I collect a sample of nasal drainage, you can go."

"If you think it's RSV, why test him?"

"Because we use different medications for viruses than we do for bacteria."

Carrie held her son in her lap while Dixie aspirated some of the fluid out of his nose and placed it in a tube of saline. Joey didn't fuss, which only proved to Dixie that he was one sick little boy.

"You can go on over to the hospital," she said. "As soon as we finish running the test, I'll notify the nurse."

"Is he going to be OK?" Carrie's voice wobbled.

"Almost everyone becomes infected with this virus before they're two years old, so it's really quite common. The thing we have to do is help Joey's immune system do its job, which means we have to treat all the bugs that have decided to attack him at the same time. It's going to take a while before you see improvement."

"But he *will* improve, won't he?"

"We'll do everything possible so that he does." Dixie patted her shoulder. "Don't worry."

Dixie carried the specimen out of the room and handed it to Miranda. "Can you test this sample for me?"

Miranda sighed. "Number twelve and it's not quite noon. Any bets on if it turns up positive?"

"Considering eight out of the eleven you've tested did, I predict the odds are good. I must say, though, Joey is the worst case I've seen this morning. Can you make arrangements for Dr Cameron to admit him?"

"Good news. You can call the hospital yourself."

"I can?"

Miranda nodded with a smile. "Mark pulled a few strings and organized emergency approval for you as an on-staff physician."

"I'm impressed."

"You should be. Once he received a faxed copy of your credentials, he didn't waste any time." She studied her carefully. "You didn't say you worked in Chicago."

"No one asked." She changed the subject because she didn't like to talk about herself. "Who should I call about Joey Jamison?"

"The admitting clerk. The extension is posted on the list by the telephone."

"Thanks." Dixie hobbled to the nearest phone and dialed the number. Seconds later, she was passing along the information about Joey.

"I'm sorry, Doctor," the woman apologized. "But we don't have any more pediatric beds."

"Then give him an adult bed. This baby needs specialized care."

"That may be, but we're full. We should have a few extra beds tomorrow."

"My patient needs one today. Not tomorrow."

"This is the best I can do. I'm sorry," she repeated.

Dixie hung up, incensed by the situation. Tucking her crutches under her arm, she thumped down the hallway in search of her boss. Luckily, she caught him coming out of a room rather than going into one, but even her mission didn't stop her from experiencing a sudden increase in her pulse rate at the sight of him in a lab coat. Although their paths hadn't crossed since he'd picked her up that morning, he was every bit as breathtaking now as he had been at eight a.m.

Breathtaking or not, Joey came first.

"I can't admit my patient," she said without preamble.

"Why not? I took care of all the paperwork so you can admit people to your heart's content."

"The problem isn't the paperwork. There aren't any beds and I have a six-month-old who's in respiratory distress."

"RSV?" he asked.

"Miranda is testing the sample as we speak, but I'll be surprised if it's negative."

He heaved a long sigh. "Did they say when a bed was available?"

"Tomorrow. Joey can't wait that long."

"Jamison?"

"Yes. Is he one of your patients?"

"Technically, he's Ned's, but I've seen him a couple of times with upper respiratory infections. His dad smokes, which doesn't help matters."

Dixie hadn't accessed the history section of Joey's computer file. After hearing his chest, she'd been more concerned about the immediate situation.

"Won't he quit, for his son's sake?"

"I've suggested it, but he assures me that he doesn't smoke in the house."

"Yeah, right. Regardless, this is another reason why I can't send that baby home until tomorrow. He needs treatment now."

Mark nodded, as if he accepted her decision. "I'll see what strings I can pull."

Without his permission, she followed him into his office and waited while he punched the number on the telephone keypad. "Did you need something else?" he asked.

"No, I just want to see how you manage to convince the admissions clerk to find a bed. I may need to borrow a few of your tactics for the next time I run into a similar situation."

He waved to the chair. "Then have a seat. This could take a while."

She sat and listened. First, he spoke to the same clerk that she had. When she didn't come through for him, he punched in a new set of numbers. "The key is to go to the top."

"Who's at the top?" she asked, curious.

"The shift nursing supervisor. She's responsible for moving patients and arranging bed space." In the next breath, he said, "Mary? It's Mark."

Dixie listened to him outline her patient's condition with a boyish charm that she hadn't expected. What she found even more intriguing was the way he smiled and laughed with the person at the other end. He looked younger, more relaxed, and less like a man who carried the weight of the world on his broad shoulders.

It didn't help to remember just how wonderful those same shoulders felt.

Neither did it help to remember that he'd visited with her last night in the same easy tone he was using now. For a while, she'd thought he'd stay longer, perhaps even share dinner with her, but he'd suddenly closed himself off. At first she'd been afraid she'd said something wrong, but for the life of her she couldn't imagine what it might have been. They'd discussed their families and her holiday schedule, none of which should have set his guard in place.

It was almost as if he'd forgotten she was Ned's cousin and her reason for being in Hope, but once he'd remembered he'd scrambled to place as much distance between them as possible. She should be grateful he was willing to let her fill in for Ned and, though she found his conditions completely unnecessary, she wouldn't complain. If she discovered that Ned's circumstances had prevented him from returning, she wouldn't have to defend him. Mark might be a hard taskmaster, but he was a fair man, and as such, he'd do the right thing when the time came.

"I knew I could count on you," he told Mary, sounding as pleased as he looked. "You're a sweetheart."

He fell silent as he listened, then laughed. "OK, Valentine's dinner is on me, but you need to make the reservations."

He was already making a date for Valentine's Day? It shouldn't bother her to know that he had someone special to take out on that night, but it did.

You're pathetic, Dixie, she told herself. Mooning over a man who had to be blackmailed in order to hire her had to rank as one of the lowest points in her life.

He replaced the receiver, grinning from ear to ear. "It's all set. Joey has a bed."

Dixie forced her thoughts onto her patient and not her colleague. If he wanted to charm the entire nursing staff, that was certainly his prerogative.

"She knows that he probably has RSV?" she persisted. "They're not going to assign him to a room with another child, are they?" The virus was highly contagious and it would defeat their purpose if he and his fellow occupant passed their germs back and forth.

"This isn't Mary's first day on the job. She knows what she's doing and, yes, it's a private room."

Even her name sounded young and pretty. Why couldn't she have been a Matilda or a Mabel?

Dixie struggled to her feet, determined to spend the rest of the afternoon at her end of the hall. She'd come to Hope to look for Ned, not to become jealous over a woman who would remain long after she herself had left. "Great. Thanks so much," she said politely.

"Any time. By the way, Jane tells me that because of you, we might be able to have lunch today."

She stopped short. "She said that?"

"Yeah. Miranda agreed. In fact, she gave me her I-told-you-so look right after she informed me that you were holding your own."

Their praise was more than Dixie had expected and, at the moment, exactly what her fragile ego needed. "I'm glad they think so. I'm not quite as fast with my knee like it is…"

"Whatever you do, don't overdo things. You're supposed to be recuperating, not working."

"I am. Recuperating, that is."

"Good. So how about lunch? There's a good soup and sandwich place a few blocks away."

With thoughts of Mary still lingering, Dixie shook her head. "I'll pass. I have a list of phone calls to make."

"About Ned?"

"I thought I'd call the cleaning services to find out if he's one of their clients."

He nodded. "OK. Maybe another day."

Fat chance! "Sure," she said, determined to pack her own lunch from then on.

Dixie headed down the hallway and stopped at the room that served as Miranda's office, their lab, and general all-purpose room. "How did Joey's test turn out?"

"Positive," Miranda said cheerfully. "Just like we thought. Did you arrange a bed for him?"

"Dr Cameron did. He worked it out with someone named Mary."

Miranda snapped her fingers. "Of course. I forgot she was working today."

Then, because she couldn't stop herself, Dixie said, "They must be good friends. He's planning to take her to dinner on Valentine's Day."

The nurse chuckled. "My sister loves to eat out. He'd better be careful or she'll set up a blind date for him."

Dixie had only heard two words. "Your sister?"

"My *older* sister, although she doesn't like it when I tell people that."

A sheepish warmth spread over Dixie's face. "I never would have guessed. They sounded so…"

"Friendly?" At Dixie's reluctant nod, Miranda explained. "When Mark first came to town, he rented one of my brother-in-law's properties and Mary took him under her wing." Her wide smile didn't hide her intent gaze. "Did you think there was something going on between them?"

Dixie shrugged helplessly and tried to stop the embarrassing flush crawl up her neck. "I didn't know. It certainly sounded as if it was possible."

Miranda chuckled. "You don't need to worry. Dr Cameron hasn't been linked to anyone since he moved here three years ago. If you're interested, the field's wide open." She winked.

"Who said I was interested?"

"Nobody. Just thought I'd share the information."

Curiosity ate at her. "What happened three years ago?"

"I suppose it wouldn't hurt to tell you," the older woman said slowly. "It certainly isn't a secret.

"He was head over heels in love with a woman who we all thought was his perfect match. He'd shown me the ring he'd bought her and, let me tell you, you practically needed sunglasses to look at it because the diamond was that big."

"What went wrong?"

"She had a gambling problem and apparently thought that marrying a doctor was the perfect way to support her habit. She admitted to searching him out for that reason. Needless to say, the ring went back to the jeweler and he never saw her again."

"How awful."

"He took the news hard and started working night and day. We finally convinced him to take a vacation last summer, but on the way back his plane crashed. He and the other doctors from town who were on board were hurt and one was killed."

Dixie wondered if that accounted for the faint scars on his face.

"After that," Miranda continued, "he decided that he should slow down, so he hired Ned." She sighed. "Sadly, that hasn't worked out too well. I don't mean to speak ill of your cousin, but Ned is as impulsive as Mark is cautious. I've never seen a young man weigh his options as much as Mark does."

Dixie thought that unusual and she said so. "How does he manage to treat his patients?"

"Believe me, when it comes to medicine, he doesn't falter

a bit. Personal matters are another story. Dr Cameron will never admit this, but I think he's lost confidence in his ability to judge character.''

"So he waits and watches.''

''Unless he's forced between a rock and a hard place.''

"Which is the only reason he hired me.''

Miranda patted her arm. ''Don't take it personally. He's glad to have you here. He just doesn't want to confess it yet. If he seems a bit moody at times, ignore him. After he mulls over everything long enough, he comes round. He always does.''

''Thanks for the advice.''

"Any time.'' Miranda glanced at the clock. ''We've cleared out the masses, so you'd better grab lunch while you can. It's hard to say what this afternoon will bring.''

Dixie didn't need a second warning. She headed for her temporary office, dug the phone book and a bottle of water out of the desk drawer and began her search of the *Yellow Pages*.

Mark leaned against the doorframe of Dixie's office and watched her as she spoke on the telephone. He could have waltzed in and sat down—her open door suggested that she wasn't having a private conversation—but he didn't mind waiting where he could enjoy the view.

Her white lab coat was crisp and neat and covered a pink blouse and navy skirt. Her short hair looked mussed, as if she'd run her hands through it a time or two.

Her voice was low and melodic and encouraging enough to inspire confidences. Yet, from the small wrinkle on her forehead and the way she rubbed the bridge of her nose, she wasn't hearing anything noteworthy.

When he'd left the building some twenty minutes ago, she'd been on the phone, too. Either Hope had far more cleaning services than he knew about or she'd discovered a number of leads and was checking them out with all the tenacity of a skilled do-or-die private investigator.

She'd surprised him in more ways than one, if the truth were known. He'd expected her to pursue the goal of locating Ned with single-minded determination and to the exclusion of all else. He'd never dreamed that she'd place the medical demands of this practice above her own, neither had he imagined that she'd care enough about his caseload to take on as many patients as she had this morning. Part of him had assumed she'd see a few token patients or cherry-pick those who had the greatest odds of knowing her cousin on a personal basis, but she'd done neither.

She'd taken each person in the order he or she had arrived and had only bypassed those who had specifically requested to see him. Mark knew that because Jane had volunteered the information and Miranda had corroborated it, although she'd done so after scolding him for leaving his new partner to sink or swim on her own. Of course, Miranda had also delighted in informing him that Dixie had functioned far better than *he* had on his first day.

If that weren't enough to impress him, knowing that she'd chosen to conduct her amateur investigation on her time and not his did. She may be related to Ned, but she certainly didn't seem to share her cousin's work ethic.

Mark's cynical nature knew that Dixie could simply be trying to get on his good side, but the idea didn't quite match with what he'd observed so far. As much as he wanted to believe that she was exactly as she appeared—conscientious and responsible—he refused to accept one morning's actions as an accurate indicator of her character. If she was as reliable as she wanted him to believe, she'd continue in the same vein throughout the rest of her time in Hope.

Idly, he glanced around the room and noticed that, other than being neat, she hadn't left her stamp on her surroundings. She hadn't even brought in a personal coffee-mug—he recognized the one on her desk as a spare they kept for special visitors. Everything in the room remained as it had before she'd arrived, although she'd moved her in-basket from the left- to the right-hand side of the desk.

The absence of food wrappers, Cellophane, crackers, or other munchies indicated that she hadn't taken time for lunch—and she probably hadn't considered it either. The only sign of her activities over the last twenty minutes was a yellow legal pad sporting a long list of names with most of them crossed out and a half a page of doodles.

Her slumped shoulders as she slipped the receiver back in its cradle suggested that she'd hit another dead end.

Taking his cue, he straightened and walked in. "Any luck?" he asked as he placed the sacks of his take-out meal on the edge of the desk.

She drew a line through another name and sighed. "Plenty. The problem is, it's all bad."

"Ned didn't hire any of the usual companies?"

Tossing her pencil on the pad, she rubbed the back of her neck. "Apparently not."

He pulled the straight-back chair out of the corner and positioned it so he faced her across her desk. "That doesn't mean he doesn't have a cleaning lady, though. Lots of women work independently. He may have hired someone like that."

"I'm already checking out some of those." Her smile was rueful. "As you can see from my list, I'm having the same kind of luck. None."

"I wouldn't worry. If this person cleans on a regular basis, you'll run into her now that you're living in his house."

"Not if she works while I'm here," she reminded him.

He dug the cartons out of the sack and placed them in a neat row. "So leave a note. If nothing else, she'll have to contact you at some point if she wants to get paid."

Her face lit up. "You're right. I hadn't thought of that." Suddenly her eyes narrowed as she focused on the plastic spoon and napkin he'd slid in her direction. "What are you doing?"

"Serving lunch."

"But I said I'd—"

"Pass," he quoted her. "I know. I heard you."

"Then why this?"

"You didn't pack a lunch. We also don't have anything to eat here unless you consider microwave popcorn a major food group. If you want enough energy to work here and still hunt for Ned, you can't run on empty." He hefted an oblong box in each hand. "Ham or turkey?"

"Turkey."

He passed it to her. "Potato soup or cream of broccoli?"

"The broccoli, please. It's my favorite."

He grinned as he slid the carton in front of her. "I thought it might be. Dig in."

At first she hesitated, then began eating with more gusto. "First breakfast and now this. You're going to spoil me."

He shrugged, unwilling to place too much emphasis on his early morning decision to provide breakfast. His craving for donuts and orange juice had had nothing to do with the vision of her empty refrigerator, or so he'd told himself. As for spoiling her, he doubted if her family had ever considered returning any of the so-called favors they demanded of her.

"I was hungry for an apple fritter this morning," he said simply. "Miranda and Jane would never forgive me if they knew I'd gone to the bakery and didn't bring donuts for them, too."

"Well, I still appreciated the thought. Ned's cupboards are running toward the bare side."

If he'd been thinking clearly last night, he would have taken her to dinner or driven her to the grocery store.

"I'm going shopping after work," she commented. "Where's the nearest supermarket?"

He gave her directions.

"Where exactly is the hospital?"

"I have a patient I want to check on after work, so you can come with me and I'll show you."

"Thanks. I'd like that since I need to see how Joey Jamison is doing."

"Did you call Peds with your orders?"

"Right before I made my other calls. I ordered lab work and a chest X-ray."

"Then they'll have the results by the time we get there," he said. "Everyone, from the nurses to the lab staff, is really good about calling us if they find anything abnormal."

"No news is good news."

"Exactly. The nurses also have a protocol to follow, which moves things along."

"This is going to be a little different for me," she said as she crumbled crackers into her soup. "I treat critical patients all the time, but then I either send them home with the proviso to see their regular physician or I turn them over to a specialist. Now I'm responsible for follow-up care."

"Won't it be nice to see their improvement for yourself?"

"Sure. As I said, it's just different."

Then, because he was curious, he asked, "Why did you choose emergency medicine?"

"I like the excitement. I'm an adrenalin junkie." She grinned before she bit into her sandwich. "And you?"

"I prefer getting to know my patients, tracking their ailments, if you will, and hopefully, heading off as many as I can. I'm also looking forward to delivering the babies of the babies I've delivered."

"Like Rosy's."

"Yes. By the way, did you know Rosy is naming her daughter Antonia?"

"Pretty name."

He grinned. "I think so. It's mine."

"Antonia?" she asked with a smile.

"Anthony," he corrected. "It's my middle name."

"It would be hard to turn Mark into something that sounded feminine, although Markanna or Markette would be unusual."

He groaned. "Please, no."

"All right. We'll scratch those. Is Antonia your first namesake?"

"Actually, she is."

"Then you'll never forget her."

"Or her arrival," he said ruefully. "I'd prefer to not deliver any more babies in my office."

She nodded. "I've delivered a few in the ER, too. While I'd rather whisk the moms to the OB floor, a normal delivery is always a nice change from the usual car accidents, gunshot wounds and stabbings."

Pausing only to blot her mouth with her napkin, she added, "That was delicious. The next lunch is on me."

"Deal." He leaned back in his chair, unwilling to leave, although from the way she was tapping her pen against her tablet she eagerly wanted to continue where she'd left off.

Mark motioned to her pad. "What's next on your plan of action?"

She flipped to a blank page and began jotting notes as she spoke. "I have two more people to contact, but if they can't help me, I'll head in another direction. The next thing to do is talk to the neighbors and his friends. Any ideas on who he hung around with in his free time?"

He shook his head. "Sorry. He never said very much about his personal life. I know he went to the junior college basketball games, but I don't think he went with anyone in particular."

"What about girlfriends? Dates, casual acquaintances?"

"Can't help you there either. He was seeing someone last fall, but it was an on-again, off-again type of relationship. I can't even remember her name. No, wait. I think her name was June, but don't hold me to it."

She sighed. "Jane and Miranda couldn't remember a name either. You mentioned going to his house for a Christmas party. Did he have a date?"

"No."

"Are you sure?"

"I think I can remember back to three weeks ago," he said dryly. "Four might be a stretch for this grumpy old man, but my brain cells can handle three."

Dixie's skin turned a becoming shade of pink. "You're never going to let me live down that comment, are you?"

He chuckled. "No. Seriously, though, he didn't have a date. He was supposed to, but I got the impression that he'd parted company with her shortly before the party. If that's the case, I doubt if he would have told her where he was going."

"I suppose not, but maybe he mentioned something to one of the nurses at the hospital."

Mark hesitated. "Before you ask too many questions, there's something you should know." At her raised eyebrow, he added, "No one, other than Jane, Miranda and myself, and the police, know that Ned has disappeared without a trace."

CHAPTER FIVE

DIXIE'S jaw dropped at Mark's announcement. "No one knows?"

"Under the circumstances, we thought it best to play everything as low-key as possible."

"Under the circumstances," she repeated. "*What* circumstances?"

He paused, as if he was carefully framing his reply. Sensing that this story was more complicated than she'd first believed or that Mark had implied, she pressed for answers.

"*What circumstances?*"

"Are you certain you want to know?"

"No, but ignoring the unpleasant doesn't make it disappear. You asked for my loyalty and for any information I might find," she reminded him. "I deserve the same courtesy."

He nodded, appearing like a man who hated the position in which he'd found himself.

"Your cousin left town," he began, "and didn't return on schedule. I was angry after days went by without a word because he knew how busy we were. Then, when he finally called to say he would be delayed, without giving an explanation, I was extremely irritated. I know that emergencies come up and we had a bad phone connection, but he could have tried calling again. For all I knew, he was simply lounging on a sunny beach, sipping margaritas and working on his tan, while I was literally snowed under with sick people."

"What made you think he was enjoying himself?" she asked, incredulous.

"I didn't at first. I changed my mind after I discovered that Ned had helped himself to twenty thousand dollars from my bank account."

Dixie's mouth fell open. She'd never been speechless before in her life, but right now words failed her. When she found her voice, she could only summarize what Mark had said and hope that she'd misunderstood. "He stole money. From you."

"From the practice account," he corrected.

"Are you sure?"

He raised one eyebrow in what was becoming a familiar gesture. "Jane may not be a CPA, but she knows how to keep the books. Both of us can also add and subtract."

"I meant, are you sure Ned took it?"

"A check was made out to cash with his signature. I have a photocopy from the bank."

"He was authorized to sign checks?"

"No one regrets that decision more than I," he said ruefully. "Last summer, before I went on vacation, we thought it would be a good idea if he had access to our bank account in an emergency. He signed the signature card, but he never used the privilege."

"Until now."

"Until now," he agreed.

"You mentioned the police. Then they know about the money?"

He nodded. "I called them as soon as we realized what Ned had done. He'll have some explaining to do when they find him."

She shook her head. "All this time… My aunt never said a word."

"She may not know. When I spoke to her, we hadn't discovered the missing money. She probably still thinks he just left town and hasn't returned."

A moment of doubt hit her. Had the police informed her aunt of this newest development and she'd simply not told Dixie? No, she decided. She'd always heard every little detail about Ned's scrapes in order to "fix" things. Withholding information wasn't the way her aunt operated.

But stealing? For what seemed like hours, Dixie tried to

assimilate this information with what she knew of Ned. Somehow, dipping his hand into his boss's till simply wasn't something she would have ever expected him to do and she said so.

"Believe it or not," he said. "I have the proof."

"And you showed that to the police?"

"Yes, I did. Either he's off having the vacation of a lifetime on money that isn't his, or…"

"Or what?"

"Or his delay means that he's somehow gotten himself into deep trouble."

Mark had mentioned Ned getting into trouble yesterday, but she'd been thinking more along the lines of the high jinks and escapades of his youth. Things like driving over the neighbor's prize azaleas with his motorcycle because he'd been late for baseball practice, or skipping school during the World Series so he could watch his favorite team win the pennant.

In college, his troubles had been more of the forgetful variety, such as losing track of his payment schedules. She'd dealt with banks and landlords to keep him from losing his car or being evicted. While those had been irritating inconveniences to her, she didn't want to think of Ned dabbling in true vice.

Like grand theft.

"There's always the possibility that he owes money to the wrong people," Mark continued. "He played poker with a high-stakes crowd on a regular basis, but I don't think this group falls in the pay-what-you-owe-or-we'll-break-your-legs category."

"That's some consolation, I suppose, but he must have had a good reason for doing what he did."

"You may not want to believe or consider that Ned might have latent criminal tendencies, but be honest. People with 'good reasons' don't help themselves to someone else's money without asking first, or at least leaving an IOU with a damn good explanation. Now, if you can think of an example of a legitimate excuse, I'd be happy to give him the benefit of the doubt. If not…''

To Dixie's disappointment, she couldn't think of one either.

''I sympathize if he's in financial trouble, but he should have gone to a bank,'' Mark added. ''I had to.''

She'd never dreamed the situation was this dire, that Ned had sunk so low. The news would destroy his mother, who'd always believed her son could do no wrong. Dixie had smoothed over enough situations to know the messenger bore the brunt of her aunt's and uncle's anger.

This time, though, Mark was paying for Ned's sins, too. From what she'd seen in the past twenty-four hours, Mark operated on a shoestring budget. Oh, he'd provided a nice environment for his patients and staff, but the whole place could use major renovation, from new paint and paneling on the walls to replacing the ancient drapes, window-blinds and flooring. Mark had clearly invested his money in the tools of his trade—his medical equipment.

Updating his building might not be in his immediate plans, but if he'd taken out a loan to cover the loss of twenty thousand dollars, he obviously didn't carry enough ready cash to cover the necessities, much less any extras.

''I'm so sorry.''

''Don't be,'' he said. ''It isn't your fault. This was Ned's decision and now it's out of my hands.''

Which meant that the police would be watching and waiting for Ned.

Dixie rubbed her temples as she tried to think. There had to be a way for her to straighten out this topsy-turvy mess, but for the life of her she couldn't see a way to accomplish it.

Unless…

Unless she didn't find Ned. Or if she found him before anyone else and gave him the opportunity to right the wrong before he returned to Hope. But by doing that, she could be accused of aiding and abetting a criminal and her own career would slide down the tubes, along with his.

Oh, Ned. How could you do this?

"I can see your mental wheels turning." Mark's gaze grew intent. "What are you thinking?"

"Nothing really…" She paused before asking, "What if he paid the money back?"

"It might keep him out of jail, but he still won't work for me. I can't trust him," he finished flatly. "And without trust, what's left?"

He was right. There *was* nothing left.

"What if I prove that you *can* trust him?"

"How? He's gone and so is my money. As far as I'm concerned, the subject is closed."

"What if there were extenuating circumstances?" she persisted. "Can't you wait to pass judgment until you have all the facts?"

She didn't waver under his silent gaze. "Fine," he admitted grudgingly. "I'll listen to Ned's side of the story, but I can't promise anything more."

As concessions went, Mark's wasn't the most encouraging, but listening was an excellent starting point. After that, actions would change his mind more than words.

"OK," she agreed, "but before we drop the subject completely, you mentioned that no one knew Ned had disappeared."

"If they know or suspect, they didn't receive that impression from us. When he didn't come back after those first few days, we simply told anyone who asked that he had a family emergency." He paused. "We certainly didn't expect a relative to come looking for him."

"So I shouldn't advertise that I'm his cousin."

"Not unless you can explain why you're not at the same family emergency."

She nodded. "As far as everyone is concerned, I'm simply your locum. And you didn't refer to the missing money?"

"The *stolen* money? No. There didn't seem any point. Ruining his reputation wouldn't solve anything."

For the first time since he'd been completely honest with

her, hope stirred within her chest. If Mark was willing to protect Ned's reputation by keeping his abrupt departure confidential, then surely, once he learned the full facts, he wouldn't balk at allowing Ned to return to his position.

Provided Ned really did have a good reason. She didn't want to think about the repercussions if he did not.

"How did the police ask questions?"

"We decided to say that the police were investigating some vandalism at his house so they wanted to know if anyone had seen unusual activity in the area or recognized any recent visitors. They also asked if Ned had made any enemies."

"So that's the story I should use?"

"Use whatever story you like. Just be aware that talking to people about Ned could backfire. The wrong question could cause people to speculate and you'll destroy the same reputation you're trying to protect."

She nodded. It would be self-defeating if she did more harm than good by asking pointed questions. "Thanks for the warning."

He rose and headed for the door, only to pause on the threshold. "I know you want to do whatever you can for him, but when will you expect him to stand on his own two feet?"

"He is," she insisted.

Disbelief crossed his face. "Then why are you so worried about him holding this job or not? Why won't you let him take his lumps like the rest of us would?"

"Because…" Her mind went blank. Why *was* she worried if Ned ruined his life? It wasn't as if his poor choices would reflect on her. And yet…

"Because he's a smart man and a talented physician, and I don't want to see that go to waste," she said firmly.

"Then let him sink or swim. On his own." He pointed to her crutches. "There's a perfect example of what you're doing to him."

"Excuse me?"

"How long are you supposed to use those?"

"A week."

"And after you've healed?"

"I ditch the crutches, take off the brace and start putting weight on my knee as much as I can tolerate."

"Exactly. There comes a point in time when you have to throw those away and rely on your leg. If you don't, if you depend on those crutches instead of strengthening your knee, you'll never recover what you lost."

The analogy fitted perfectly, although quite painfully. "I suppose."

"So stop being Ned's crutch. As you said, he's a talented physician. There's no reason for you to fight his battles, especially when he's started them himself. If he handles his own problems without outside interference, he may surprise you with what he can accomplish." With that parting shot, he left.

She'd never considered that what she was doing for Ned, what she *had* done for Ned over the years, had enabled him to remain weak in certain areas of his life. As Dixie eyed the aluminum crutches propped against her desk, she faced the unwelcome truth Mark had uncovered and wondered why the idea of withholding her support seemed like such a betrayal…

"Last stop, Peds." Mark guided Dixie out of the intensive care unit toward the double doors separating the east wing from the west. Conscious of her slow gait, he'd shortened his stride to accommodate hers. Normally, he rushed from place to place, but today the nurses couldn't tease him about heading toward a fire. With Dixie at his side, he couldn't dash through the hospital, but even if that were possible, he wasn't in any hurry to exchange her company for the gilled variety waiting for him at home.

"What do you think of our ICU?" he asked.

"It's impressive for its size."

Although he hadn't expected her to rave about their intensive care unit or to be particularly awed by it, he had expected her to show a little more interest.

"Four beds may not be many when you're used to rows and rows of critical patients," he said mildly, determined not to take offense when he knew she'd been preoccupied all afternoon, "but we're proud of our department. We've worked hard to stock it with state-of-the-art equipment."

"I wasn't finding fault," she apologized. "Honest. It's plain that your administration is providing the best to your patients, regardless of the cost. You definitely should be proud of your ICU. I'm sorry if I gave the impression that 'small' meant 'substandard.'"

She sighed. "Maybe today wasn't the best day for a tour. I have too many other things on my mind."

"I know." He also knew he was partly to blame. She might have been disappointed by the dead ends she'd encountered in her amateur investigation, but she hadn't lost the sparkle in her eyes until he'd attacked the way she rode to Ned's rescue. He stood by his opinion—that she should let Ned crawl out of the hole he'd dug—but hindsight told Mark that he should have used a softer approach.

While he might not know if she planned to take his advice, he was certain of one thing. The swish of her skirt and her subtle fragrance was driving him mad. If he allowed himself to think about the wisps of silk he'd seen in her suitcase, he'd find the nearest empty closet and kiss her until her toes curled.

As quick as a wink, he realized how close he'd come to never meeting her. If Ned hadn't disappeared, or if he hadn't moved to Hope last fall, their paths would never have crossed. So, in spite of the catastrophes of the last two weeks, Mark felt somewhat indebted to his colleague. With that sort of cosmic tie, it seemed strange, in a fate-defying sort of way, to wish that Ned wouldn't return. He may have promised Dixie that he'd listen to Ned's tale, but he truly didn't believe Ned had a legitimate reason for his actions.

All of which meant that when Ned waltzed back into town, Mark would literally crush Dixie's feelings when he pressed charges against her cousin.

Although he hated to think of Ned exchanging his medical career for a jail sentence, Ned deserved what he got. If he stole that much money and got away without anything more than a slap on the wrist, what would he try next?

No, dealing with Ned was only a minor pothole in Mark's road of life. Recouping his losses was a little more serious roadblock and would require some major readjustments in his plans, but doing so would be more of a setback than an insurmountable problem. The true sticky situation lay with Dixie herself.

He'd only known her for twenty-four hours, but he hadn't been able to shake her out of his mind since the moment he'd caught her going through Ned's desk. Maybe if she hadn't felt so damn good plastered against him, he wouldn't care if she watched her cousin being led away in handcuffs. But he did care, and he couldn't bear knowing that he'd caused her pain.

He hadn't met anyone in years who had remotely triggered his romantic interest and now that he had, he wanted to explore that attraction. Yet how far could a relationship develop with Ned's situation casting such a long shadow over it? She'd never forgive him if he insisted on Ned receiving his due.

Ned obviously didn't appreciate or understand the depth of Dixie's loyalty and that alone irked Mark no end. The man was snubbing the very thing that Mark wanted for himself. Several years ago, he'd thought he'd found his dream with Andrea, but her loyalty had rested with her gambling habit and not with him. He'd merely been a means to an end.

Now Mark had to walk a fine line between seeking justice and shielding Dixie from her cousin's indiscretions.

"Mark? Hello?"

"What?" Realizing she'd asked him a question, he grinned sheepishly. "Sorry. I was woolgathering."

"Don't we all at one time or another?" she asked simply, making it sound more like a statement than a question.

"What did you want to know?"

"I just wondered why they'd placed Pediatrics and ICU on the same floor."

"Couldn't tell you," he said. "With all the tonsillectomies and myringotomies that we do here, I would think peds patients should be closer to the same-day surgery unit."

"Maybe someone wanted the kids tucked away because of the noise."

"Could be. At least they have a ward to themselves. The old-timers have told me the children used to be slotted in with the general population, so we've made some progress."

He pushed the heavy fire door and held it open for Dixie to maneuver through. "Do you know what room Joey is in?"

"No."

"Then we'll stop at the nurses' station," he said, leading the way.

The head nurse, Rebecca Roberts, sat behind the desk. She was in her early forties and wasn't much taller than her patients, but she wore a perpetual smile and was a picture of calm whether she had two patients or twenty.

"Slow day?" he teased.

Rebecca glanced up from her chart and chuckled as she motioned to the pile waiting for her attention. "How did you guess?" she asked. "You must be here for Joey."

"Actually, he's Dr Albright's patient," Mark said smoothly before he introduced the two, took Dixie's coat and draped it over a chair.

Immediately impressed by the nurse's friendly manner, Dixie accepted the thin chart Rebecca handed over without prompting on her part. "How's he doing?"

"We wore him out completely," she answered. "Respiratory gave him an albuterol treatment as soon as he arrived because I could tell the poor thing was really struggling for air. We also had a devil of a time starting his IV, but we managed. His labs are posted on the chart, along with his X-ray report. His films are next to the viewbox, by the way. I asked Radiology to send them along in case you wanted to see them for yourself."

Dixie did. "Thanks."

"I'll take you to his room whenever you're ready."

After acknowledging the nurse's comment with a nod, Dixie glanced through the record. Little Joey was dehydrated—his electrolytes were out of balance, as she'd suspected—and his chest X-ray showed a diffuse pattern of inflammation. His white count was elevated, too, which pointed to bacterial causes, although it was hard to say if those bugs were the primary or secondary source of his infection. With his RSV test positive, the poor little guy faced a long battle even with all the drugs at their disposal.

"Continue the fluids and the antibiotics," she said as she scribbled her orders. "Breathing treatments every four hours and keep him in the tent." The plastic tent over the crib allowed them to create a high-oxygen, high-humidity environment that helped to relieve chest congestion without turning the entire room into a tropical rain forest.

"Did you want to start an antiviral med?"

Dixie knew that studies on the drug's killing effects against this virus were mixed, but Joey fell in the high-risk category of being less than a year old.

"I believe we should." She turned toward Mark, surprised to see him sprawled in a chair as if he had nothing in the world to do. "What do you think?"

"You're the doctor."

She wrote the order for respiratory therapy to administer the drug via aerosol. "Monitor him for any side effects," she said as she signed her name.

"Will do."

Dixie glanced down at Mark. "Do you want to join me?"

"I have faith in you," he said, making no effort to move. "This is the first time I've been off my feet since lunch, so I'd rather not get up until I have to."

His confidence suddenly restored her flagging spirits. After learning about Ned's perfidy and digesting Mark's comment about being Ned's crutch, she hadn't been in the best of moods. Truth was often a painful pill to swallow, even if it was prescribed with the best intentions.

"Suit yourself," she said.

Dixie walked to the room directly across from the nurses' station, aware of Mark's gaze following her. She wished she wasn't quite so clumsy with her crutches, or so slow, but he hadn't complained during his tour of the hospital or acted as if he'd wanted her to hurry. In any event, she felt more self-conscious than self-assured.

Inside the room, she couldn't see much improvement in Joey's condition, but mothers were often a better guide to their child's response than doctors. "How's he doing?" she asked softly, in deference to Joey's exhausted sleep.

"About the same," Carrie admitted as she stroked her son's arm above his IV. "I think the breathing treatment helped a little, though."

"He'll be getting those every few hours, and once the antibiotic takes hold in the next twenty-four hours, he'll start to bounce back."

"My husband wants to know how long Joey will be here."

"It's hard to say. Every child responds differently. Several days, at least." Dixie glanced around the room. "Did he come with you?"

"He's downstairs," Carrie admitted. "He gets nervous in hospitals, so he went to smoke a cigarette."

Dixie mentally filed away the information. "Maybe I'll catch him next time. If you have any questions or concerns, talk to the nurses. They'll call me if Joey takes a turn for the worse. Otherwise, I'll see him in the morning."

In the hallway near the nurses' station, Dixie pulled Rebecca aside and spoke in a low voice. "I want a urine specimen collected for a cotinine level."

"Never heard of it," Rebecca said. "What is it?"

"Cotinine is a breakdown product of nicotine. It's positive in smokers and those who've been exposed to secondhand smoke."

"Ah," the nurse nodded knowingly. "I'll warn you, though. I doubt if our lab tests for it on site and if they don't, it will take several days to get a result."

"I understand, but impress on them that if it's at all possible, I want the figures before Joey goes home."

"Yes, ma'am."

Dixie stopped in front of Mark. "I'm ready if you are." At the sudden gleam in his eyes, she added, "To leave."

"Did you mean something else?" he asked innocently as he helped her with her coat.

"Never mind."

As he followed her to the elevator, he said, "I overheard you order a cotinine level."

She stopped and rested on her crutches. "Is that a problem?"

"Not with me. I assume you're going to use Joey's results to convince his father to stop smoking."

"If he doesn't light up inside the house, he has nothing to worry about, does he?"

"Hey!" He raised his hands. "I'm all for doing whatever it takes to ensure that Joey has clean air to breathe. I only wish I'd thought of it myself. Brilliant strategy, Dr Albright."

She'd expected him to talk her out of her order, not endorse it. "We won't know how brilliant it is until the results come in, but it's worth a try."

"'Nothing ventured, nothing gained,'" he quoted.

Once they'd reached the front door on the main level, he said, "Where to next?"

"Home."

"Big plans?"

She chuckled. "Not unless you consider a quick trip to the store as a 'big plan.' My day doesn't start right if I don't fall into my bowl of cornflakes every morning."

"I was going there myself. I'll give you a ride."

She didn't know if she should be flattered or irritated. "I can manage. I'm not crippled."

"We'll meet each other there anyway," he said, sounding maddeningly practical. "You aren't the only one with a Mother Hubbard cupboard, so we may as well carpool."

She truly did appreciate his offer. Not only would she

shorten the number of hours she spent alone with her thoughts and her list at Ned's house, but spending time with Mark didn't rate as any hardship. In fact, she couldn't think of anyone with whom she'd rather spend a few more hours.

"I don't want you to go to any trouble," she said, trying not to sound over-eager.

"No trouble. Do you mind if we stop at our Italian restaurant first? They serve a buffet on Tuesday nights that is perfect for starving doctors like me."

"You ate lunch, remember?"

"Yes, but I've had a busy afternoon. Burned a lot of calories."

She laughed. "OK, dinner and grocery shopping. I still think I should drive myself, in case you get called to the hospital."

"We'll worry about that if it happens."

And with that, the activities and logistics for the evening were settled.

Donatelli's was packed, but Mark managed to find an intimate table for two in one corner. He'd also insisted on filling a plate for her, and when he returned with a platter piled high, she laughed aloud.

"Do you honestly expect me to eat that much?"

"It's a requirement to taste everything," he said. "The cook will feel slighted if you don't."

She picked up her fork. "You'll have to roll me out of here if I finish this."

His eyes flared with an emotion she could only describe as hungry. She'd seen it when her friends' boyfriends looked at them, but it was exhilarating to be on the receiving end of such a glance.

"Somehow I doubt it," he said before he twirled spaghetti around his fork. "How long are you going to be on crutches, did you say?"

"Technically, I don't have to use them after the stitches come out on Thursday."

"What exactly happened?"

"I fell on a patch of ice early one morning outside the hospital. I twisted my knee and although it was horribly swollen, I wasn't too worried."

"I hope you consulted Orthopedics."

"Not then," she admitted. "I babied it along, and did quite well until my knee occasionally started locking. I saw the head of the orthopedics department and he suggested an arthroscopy. I agreed, because if the problem was simple, they could repair the damage at the same time."

"Which they obviously did."

She nodded. "When it was over, the orthopedic surgeon said the procedure had been straightforward and I'd be back on my feet in no time."

"And your knee brace?"

"That will come off on Thursday also. I'm wearing it longer than I need to, but I'd rather err on the side of caution. In another week or two, I expect to have full range of motion again."

"You shouldn't be working, should you?"

"I'm supposed to wait four to six weeks before I return to heavy work or sports, but since I'm not a construction worker or an athlete, I'm fine."

"Yet you took a month off."

"I was only going to take this week, but with Ned..." She didn't finish that sentence. "Anyway, I had earned enough time off that I was going to lose it if I didn't use it, so I decided this was a good opportunity to whittle down my banked hours."

"Are you driving back to Chicago on Thursday?"

"Hardly," she said wryly. "I'm sure the ER doctor here can do the honors with my knee. I'd do it myself if I wasn't such a wimp."

"You? A wimp?" His eyes sparkled with merriment.

"Oh, yes. I can dish pain out but I can't take it." She grinned. "On the other hand, I work for a grumpy old boss who may not let me off to go to the ER."

"You're right. He may not," he agreed with a chuckle.

"He'll just have to do the job himself. To make sure it's done right, of course."

"Of course. By the way, have any interesting applicants contacted you?"

"Interesting, yes. Suitable, no. I'll keep looking. You wouldn't happen to know of anyone who'd like to move to a small town with a thriving practice and a progressive hospital?"

"Not off the top of my head, but if you haven't found anyone, I'll ask around when I go back to Chicago."

For the first time since she'd come to Hope, she realized that she wasn't eager to return to her familiar stomping grounds.

What a difference a mere twenty-four hours made.

No, that wasn't quite right. Time hadn't made the difference at all. It was the man seated across the table from her who could claim sole responsibility for her sudden discontent. This attractive, sometimes overbearing and bossy but refreshingly gallant man had shown her how empty her life in Chicago really was, and he didn't even know he'd done so.

Suddenly, she wasn't as eager to find Ned as she had been when she'd arrived. The common goal of Mark and herself finding Ned allowed her to spend time with the handsome doctor that she otherwise wouldn't have had, and every day's delay meant one more day in Hope. One more day of dreaming that she wasn't alone.

She'd almost be willing to let something develop between them, but fear held her back. In spite of her faith in her cousin, deep down she was afraid that it might be misplaced. And if it was, any relationship she developed with Mark in the interim would wither and die after the painful truth was revealed.

And that would be the biggest disappointment of all.

CHAPTER SIX

"WOULD you like a cup of hot chocolate?" Dixie asked as soon as Mark returned from de-icing Ned's porch that same evening. She'd tried to tell him that he'd done enough for her after he'd carried in her groceries and doubled-checked the new garage door opener to be sure it worked, but he'd insisted.

So while he'd braved the cold once again, she'd quickly made hot chocolate. She'd tried to tell herself that she was only showing hospitality. That she merely wanted to repay him in some small way for everything he'd done when he could have left her to fend for herself. That sending him back into the cold without giving him an opportunity to warm up was cruel and heartless.

She knew otherwise. While those excuses were true to a certain degree, her real reason was that she simply didn't want their evening to end.

"I'd love one." He pulled off his leather gloves and stuffed them into his coat pocket before he dumped his coat on a kitchen chair.

"Have a seat," she said, forcing her gaze off his sweater-clad shoulders and onto the cocoa as she filled two mugs.

Instead of doing so, he approached her and peered over her shoulder. "Is that home-made?"

He smelt of fresh air and a hint of spice, and she cautioned herself not to act like a flighty teenager.

"That's right," she said, pleased that her voice sounded normal in spite of her heart skipping in her chest. "Once in a while, I splurge and fix the real stuff." Fortunately, the idea had come to her in the grocery store so she'd purchased all the ingredients in case the opportunity arose.

"Wow. I can't remember the last time I had made-from-real-milk hot chocolate." He sniffed. "Smells good."

She plopped a handful of the mini-marshmallows she'd bought in each cup, then slid one in front of him. "Enjoy."

"I will." He wrapped his hands around the mug as she took hers and limped to the table.

"Are you supposed to be walking without your crutches?" he asked, his gaze pointedly moving toward the spot where she'd propped them against the counter.

"My orthopedist said I could bear weight as tolerated, so I decided to start warning my leg of what to expect in two more days." She sat, trying to hide her relief at being off her feet. "Besides, my arms were tired."

"Don't overdo it."

"I won't, but speaking of overdoing things, you really should let me take my share of call-back."

"We'll talk about it next week."

She bristled at his dismissive tone. "I'm serious. There is no reason why you should handle the needs of the practice twenty-four seven while I'm here."

"I know."

"Then why won't you?"

"If you think I'm dumping the responsibility on you after one day on the job, you can think again. We'll talk about it on Monday."

He didn't need to add, *and that's final*, because she heard it quite clearly in his tone.

"Monday," she agreed.

"Any luck on the mystery housekeeper?"

"No."

"I presume no one at the hospital was much help either."

She shook her head. "I only talked to a few nurses in OB while you were busy with Rosy Valesquez and her baby. It's hard to ask questions when you have to watch every word."

"I wouldn't worry too much. When you least expect it, you'll run across someone who can give you another piece to the puzzle. So tell me what you do in your spare time in Chicago.''

He clearly didn't want to discuss Ned and, to be honest, neither did she. ''I have season tickets to the Chicago Symphony. Then there are trips to the Shedd Aquarium or just strolling along the Navy Pier to feel the breeze coming off the lake.''

''So you like water?''

''I don't know that I like it,'' she said. ''Fascinated might be a better word. No.'' She shook her head. ''That's not right either. Cautiously curious. My parents drowned, you know.''

''I'm sorry,'' he murmured. ''What happened?''

''A boating accident on the lake. Until I became a teenager, I couldn't be around anything larger than a pool. When I was sixteen, I forced myself to take control of my fear instead of allowing it to control me, so I started visiting the aquarium. I finally saw that the water held life in it, too, not just death, and then I was able to move on.'' She grinned to lighten the suddenly serious mood. ''Now I teach lifesaving classes at the YMCA.''

''I'm impressed.''

''It's all mind over matter.''

''You make it sound so easy.''

''It wasn't, believe me.''

''Did your aunt and uncle help you deal with this, too?''

She skirted the issue. It was one thing to know that they'd taken her in on sufferance and another to admit it to anyone else. ''They had their own problems,'' she said simply. ''I tried not to dump any of mine on them, too.''

Then, because she preferred to talk about something other than herself, she changed the subject. ''As for things to do, the fantastic restaurants are a special outing in themselves.''

''Never a dull moment, I suppose.''

''No,'' she confessed, ''but not for the reasons you might imagine. I work ten- and twelve-hour shifts on a good day. After I come home, a night on the town doesn't cross my mind.''

"What about your days off?"

"There's so much to see and do that I barely scrape the tip of the iceberg with the few things I've already mentioned." She grinned. "And everyone knows I'm a sucker for a hard-luck story. If anyone wants to attend their kid's soccer game or ballet recital, they ask me to fill in."

"And you accommodate them."

"Usually." She shrugged. "I'm hoping that when I have children, someone will do the same for me."

"Planning on starting a family soon?" he asked mildly.

"Someday," she replied.

"My grandmother always told me that someday never comes."

"Smart woman." Then, because her love life was fairly dismal at the moment, she focused on his empty cup. "More hot chocolate?"

"I can help myself."

"No," she insisted, rising. "My house, my rules."

"I don't have a gimpy leg," he said.

"Humor me." She poured the last of the hot drink into their mugs and topped each with marshmallows before returning to the table. "What do the locals do for fun in Hope?"

He sipped, then licked the foam off his upper lip. "Let's see…"

Focused on his mouth, Dixie's temperature rose a few degrees, along with her blood pressure. The temptation to kiss him was strong, but she gripped the handle of her mug to restrain herself.

"We have a bowling alley," he said. "Then there's dinner and dancing at several of the bars. If you're into athletics, the health club has tennis and handball courts."

"A swimming pool?" she asked, remembering her Valentine's wish.

He nodded. "Yeah. Along with a hot tub and sauna. If you prefer checking out Lady Luck, the city band members host a bingo parlor on the first and third Saturday nights of the month. It's only open during the winter, though."

"I thought bingo was a year-round activity."

"It is. The guys hold free concerts on the courthouse square in the summer, so they don't have time for anything else. If you want to hear something more unusual, though, you should hear Annie Tremaine."

"What does she play?"

"Bagpipes. When the weather and her schedule permits, she performs at the fire station. She draws quite a crowd, too."

"I'd love to hear her."

"It's too cold right now, but once May arrives, she'll be outside entertaining the neighborhood. You won't want to miss it."

She didn't want to, but logic reminded her that she would. Once she resolved Ned's situation, or her month came to a close, she would leave. And if Ned didn't work in Hope, she couldn't return under the guise of visiting him. Maybe if Ned stayed, she would, but Mark had made his feelings about his professional association with her cousin quite plain. Unless fate granted her a miracle, she'd never enjoy Annie's performance.

"Sounds like fun," she answered noncommittally.

He took a long swallow of his hot chocolate. "This is really great. How did you make it? Milk and chocolate and what else?"

"Family secret. If I told you, I'd have to—"

"Marry me?"

She'd planned to finish her statement along the lines of what a spy might say, but Mark's suggestion presented a far more tantalizing prospect.

"Absolutely," she assured him with a smile. "With no chance of ever getting a divorce either."

"Some might say you were asking a steep price."

Their conversation had suddenly assumed a double meaning. No matter. She didn't care who knew that she considered marriage to be a lifetime commitment and not just a we'll-stay-together-until-someone-better-comes-along sort of relationship.

"Things worth having are worth paying for," she said lightly. "My great-grandmother took her family recipes seriously, which is why they're only passed down through the women. She believed in the adage of the way to a man's heart being through his stomach, and I think she was determined to give the future generations of girls an edge."

He chuckled, then drained the last of his cocoa. "For cocoa like that, she was right. Are we still on for Thursday night?"

Thursday was her enchilada night. "Yes."

"I don't suppose hot chocolate goes with Mexican food," he said, sounding hopeful.

"No." She laughed at his crestfallen face. "I'll serve it after dinner, though."

"Ah," he said, plainly satisfied. "One more thing to look forward to."

One *more* thing? She hoped he wasn't only talking about food—she wanted his list to include being in her company.

He rose and carried his mug to the sink, and she did the same. "I should be going. Thanks again."

"My pleasure." She noticed a dab of marshmallow goo on the corner of his upper lip and blotted the spot away with her napkin.

It was completely unplanned—one of those instinctive things one did for a child or a husband, not for a casual acquaintance or a colleague. She realized her mistake as soon as she'd made it, but she couldn't rewind time.

Her familiarity surprised him as much as it did her. His eyes looked as startled as she felt, and she was quite relieved that he didn't recoil. For a few seconds, though, she was positive that neither of them breathed.

She couldn't ask for a rerun—life was firm about those. Instead, she could only backpedal and treat the incident—and him—as if her action had been too inconsequential to think about.

"Marshmallow," she explained. "It's gone now."

If she'd stepped back and turned away, the sudden aware-ness that had flashed between them the instant she'd touched his mouth would have disappeared as quickly as it had flared into existence. That was all it would have taken.

But she couldn't budge. Her feet had become rooted to the floor and her knees had locked into position. If that weren't enough of a response, her pulse rate had doubled and a long-ing ache in her chest grew to enormous proportions.

She wanted to feel his arms slide around her, to feel his body pressed against hers. She was desperate to taste the chocolate on his lips, and so very eager to surround herself with his warmth.

He must have seen the yearning on her face, because his answering gaze held a desire that plainly matched hers. His hand crept up to cup the side of her face a mere instant before his other hand did the same.

Then, as frustration at his delay started to build until she was afraid she couldn't stand it any longer, he closed the half-step between them and kissed her.

His mouth was gentle for only a second before he suddenly pulled her against him. A guttural sound came from his throat before he unleashed enough emotion to literally steal her breath and good sense away.

She clung to him, unable and unwilling to do anything else. This was where she wanted to be—in his arms, wrapped in his embrace.

A reaction this powerful should have built up over time, or so she'd always told herself. Instant chemistry was a flash in the pan, a fireworks display that burned quickly and then was gone. However, Mark had disproved all of her ideas. It didn't matter that she'd only met him a short time ago because it seemed as if she'd known him for ever.

"Mark," she managed to say, wanting to say more and unable to form the words. Somehow, and much to her delight, he understood that she needed his touch as much as she needed air.

His mouth trailed along the sensitive column of her neck

and his hands slowly roamed across her curves as if he were charting a reference map. As he touched her breast, she felt like the mythical phoenix that rose above the ashes of its previous form, completely and utterly transformed into new life. Never again would she be satisfied with anything less than the sparks she now experienced.

And she wanted to return the favor—to give to him a measure, at least, of what he'd given her. She wanted him more than she'd ever wanted anyone before.

Her sudden realization jolted her back to her senses. She didn't lose herself in a guy after knowing him for one day. Her instincts might claim that he was exactly as he appeared, that he wasn't feeding her a line in order to scratch a temporary itch, but she still didn't fall into a guy's bed after such a short acquaintance.

For one thing, she wanted more. Flitting from relationship to relationship was too difficult for her. She wanted stability, a family that she could nurture, and she wanted it with a man like Mark. A man of principle. A man of honor. A man of high standards who refused to compromise. Falling for him would be so easy.

And, thanks to Ned, so complicated.

She drew back and frantically tried to salvage what she could out of the situation. "That was…" She drew a blank as if his kiss had completely emptied her brain of all rational thought.

"Powerful?" he suggested, his gaze intent.

She could think of all sorts of wonderful adjectives, but "foolish" headed the list.

"Yeah," she said instead, glad that he hadn't chosen a word like "regrettable." No matter what happened, or didn't as the case might be, she didn't regret a single second.

Then, because the best way to avoid all sorts of explanations and apologies was to hide behind humor, she did.

"I know you want my cocoa recipe," she said lightly, "but I can't hand it over on the basis of a mere kiss."

His serious dark-eyed gaze bored into her. "There was nothing 'mere' about it."

She thought about denying the truth, but couldn't. If he obviously felt the same one-two punch that she did, he deserved an honest answer.

"No," she agreed.

"So what happens next?"

"Nothing." Her voice sounded weak and she cleared her throat before she repeated herself. "Nothing."

"Nothing?"

"It wouldn't be the smart thing to do," she amended.

"Even if it feels right?"

Her resolve wavered. It wasn't every day that she met a man who shifted her world off its axis.

"I won't deny that I'm attracted to you," she said, aware of a blush spreading its heat across her face, "but if we acted on that...think of the complications we'd face."

"What's complicated? We connect in ways that a lot of people don't. That's pretty unusual."

"It is, but we work together, which is the best way to ruin a romantic relationship." She forestalled his objection with a raised hand. "Secondly, I could leave tomorrow."

"You won't." He crossed his arms and looked at her with complete certainty.

"Tomorrow is a bit of an exaggeration," she admitted, "but the point is, I'm not here for the long haul."

"A kiss doesn't make a commitment," he pointed out. "Why not enjoy each other's company for the time you're here and for as along as we *do* enjoy being together?"

She left what she considered as the biggest drawback for last. "How do we get around Ned?"

"This doesn't involve him. It's between you and me. No one else."

She wanted to believe that with all her heart, but she managed to raise one last objection. "Regardless of our reasons, we're both trying to find him. We can't afford to be distracted from our goal."

He bridged the short distance she'd placed between them. "I hate to tell you this," he growled, "but I'm already distracted."

His breath brushed across her cheek and it was only sheer willpower on her part that kept her out of his arms. "You are?"

"Thoroughly," he assured her. "As for finding Ned, I hate to burst your bubble, but we're not going to see him until he wants to be seen."

He sounded so certain, and therein lay the problem. Mark had a far more jaundiced view of her cousin than she did.

"You promised to be open-minded," she reminded him.

"I said I'd listen to him and I will."

"But—"

"Let's agree to disagree on this subject and leave it at that, shall we?"

"That's my point. I'm not sure I can."

He paused. "Then you're willing to ignore what's between us?"

Was she willing? No.

"I have to," she said miserably.

For a few seconds Mark didn't move. He couldn't. If he moved as much as a muscle, he'd pull her back into his arms and he knew he shouldn't. Her answer was no and that was that, even if he didn't like it.

If he was a smart man, he'd be grateful for the excuses she'd handed him. For a man who'd taken caution to new limits since his fiasco with Andrea, he must be losing his mind to pursue a woman he hardly knew with such single-minded purpose.

This was a test, he justified. Only a test. He'd been afraid she would resort to any tactic and use him in any way to ensure that Ned didn't lose his job. What better way to make it easy for her to do so?

If it was a test, it backfired, something inside informed him.

How true, he admitted wryly. Not only did he feel things he'd never felt with Andrea, but Dixie had passed with flying colors. She appeared too sincere and too apologetic in her refusal to be acting.

But could he be wrong? He'd been wrong before—both Andrea and Ned had seemed sincere, too. Circumstances being what they were, he really didn't have any business getting involved with Dixie. Logic demanded that he step on the brakes and approach this as warily as he had in the past, but if he was honest with himself, he was just plain tired of being cautious.

No one knew he felt that way, of course. Facing his own mortality last summer had caused him to think about the things he was missing in his life, but Richmond's retirement and bringing Ned on board had kept him too busy to focus on his personal life.

Now, when he'd least expected it, along came a woman who was the first one in ages to make him feel alive. A year ago, he would have ignored those feelings, but now he refused to let her go without a fight. Anything worth having was worth fighting for, even if it only lasted for a season.

"Last summer, my plane crash-landed not far from town," he said idly as he tugged on his coat and gloves. "During those minutes of terror, I realized a couple of things. The first was that life is precarious and far too short.

"The second was that when my time came, I didn't want to have more regrets than I already do." He met her gaze. "In case you don't know, they don't make the best companions."

He walked outside, hoping that time alone would make her rethink her decision. Otherwise he would be taking a lot of cold showers and spending a lot of time shoveling snow.

"What's going on around here?" Miranda asked on Thursday afternoon.

"What do you mean?" Dixie asked, somewhat puzzled. As far as she knew, everything was running as usual.

"Dr Cameron has been walking around like a bear with a sore head for the past two days. Any particular reason why?"

"Not that I can say," she prevaricated.

"Then would you mind finding out what bee is in his bonnet? Jane and I are going to go on strike if he doesn't straighten up."

Remorse filled Dixie. She knew exactly why Mark was being difficult. In deference to her wishes, he'd backed away from her and the frustration was driving him mad.

"I'll talk to him," she promised, although she didn't know quite what to say. "I don't know if it will do any good, though."

"As long as you try," Miranda said gratefully. "That's all we ask."

Dixie leaned back in her chair and stared through the window. Mark wasn't the only one in their small office who was frustrated. She'd replayed their conversation until it haunted her. After two days of thinking, hashing and rehashing her options, it was quite plain that ignoring her attraction to Mark topped her long list of regrets.

It would have been far simpler if she hadn't known the feeling was mutual, although even if he hadn't said a word she might have guessed. His smoldering gaze, his quirky little half-smile, and the occasional questioning eyebrow reflected his thoughts perfectly.

She was in deep trouble.

Although he hadn't said another word, her own conscience was wearing her down. What would it hurt to be with a man who looked at her as if the sun rose and set in her? Why *couldn't* she enjoy the attentions of an attractive man? She hadn't taken any vows of celibacy.

As for her limited stay in Hope, some of her friends had fallen in and out relationships in less time.

So why was she holding back? A relationship with Mark was the very thing she wanted, the very thing she dreamed of having, regardless of how far it progressed.

She answered her own question. Chemistry wasn't enough. She wanted the love, the passion, the soul connection between two people. Other people had those things and she wanted them, too. Never having received or experienced that special bond before, she refused to short-change herself by accepting anything less.

And yet, for those first years after her parents had died, she had dreamed… Dreamed of being back with them, feeling her mom's warm hugs and hearing her dad's teasing comments and off-key singing about his little Dixie. Later, those dreams had come less frequently, but when she felt so low that she thought she'd never smile again, she'd dust off those dreams, clutch them to her chest and promise herself that she'd have those again. Someday.

Miranda knocked on the door. ''Sorry to interrupt. I know you're between patients and doing your paperwork, but a patient just came in who concerns me.''

Eager to concentrate on something other than her personal dilemma, Dixie asked, ''What's wrong?''

''It's Opal Landers. I've known her for years and she just isn't acting right. She seems disoriented and unsteady, which is surprising because she was just here a week ago and was perfectly fine.''

''Maybe Dr Cameron should examine her.''

''He went to the hospital about an hour ago and isn't back yet. Maybe I'm overreacting, but I don't think Opal should wait, unless you say so.''

Dixie rose, tucked one crutch under her right armpit and headed for the door. ''Symptoms?''

''Her pupils are reacting unevenly, she's unsteady on her feet and she's complaining about a headache.''

''Blood pressure?''

''Elevated, but not through the roof. Something is going on, though I don't have anything to go on except my instinct.''

Dixie had learned not to discount a nurse's observations, especially one with Miranda's experience. ''How old is she?''

''Seventy-two.''

''Any signs of trauma?''

''I thought of that so I checked. None.''

"Did you ask her?"

Miranda nodded. "She denied it. So did her daughter."

"Does she live alone or with her family?"

"Alone, although Karen Haffner, her daughter, usually spends the morning with her."

Dixie paused outside the door. "OK. Let's take a look." She opened the cubicle door to find a white-haired lady sitting on the exam table and her fortyish daughter occupying a nearby chair.

"I'm Doctor Albright," Dixie introduced herself as she entered the room. "Dr Cameron went to the hospital and because we're not sure how long he'll be delayed, Miranda asked me to check on you. Do you mind seeing a different doctor today?"

"Of course not, dearie," Opal said in a quivery voice.

"Now, what can you tell me?" Dixie asked as she began to check her patient's neurological status.

"My mother's been acting strange all morning," Karen reported. "Before I brought her here, she started walking as if she were drunk. And she's developed a tremor in her right hand."

Dixie had noticed it, too, including the way Opal avoided her gaze.

"I have a headache and need to rest," Opal interjected tartly. "After that, I'll be as good as new."

Karen ignored her mother and continued. "She got up, ate breakfast like always, insisted on carrying her own laundry downstairs—"

Opal sniffed. "I'm still capable of throwing my own clothes in the washing-machine."

"I know you are, Mother," Karen said tiredly. "I'm just trying to help."

"Did you take any medication this morning?"

"My vitamins, blood thinner and a cholesterol pill."

Dixie continued her exam, gently running her fingers over Opal's scalp. To her surprise, when she touched an area on the top of Opal's head, the older woman winced.

"Mrs Haffner," Dixie said offhandedly, "would you mind stepping outside for a few minutes while we finish your mother's exam?"

Although clearly puzzled and surprised by Dixie's request, Karen rose. "OK," she said, sounding wary. "I'll wait in the hall."

Dixie fixed a smile on her face, though she found the situation troubling. She had a feeling that Opal might be more forthcoming if she could speak freely. "Thanks. We won't be long."

As soon as the door latch snicked behind Karen and left the three of them alone, Dixie went straight to the heart of the matter. "I notice you have a sore spot on the top of your head."

Opal waved away her comment with one age-spotted, arthritic hand. "It's nothing."

Dixie gently parted the lady's hair to find a purplish bruise about the size of a golf ball. "This looks extremely painful."

"It is. I bumped myself."

Dixie exchanged a glance with Miranda. "How?"

"Does it matter?"

"Yes, it does," Dixie replied gently, already wondering if Opal's symptoms were due to a possible subdural hematoma.

Opal sighed. "It's really quite silly. I'd opened the silverware drawer to put away the utensils and I dropped a spoon. After I picked it up and started to straighten, I forgot about the drawer and ran my head into the corner."

Opal sounded so disgusted with herself that Dixie believed her. She had seen the V-shaped mark and, with abuse of the elderly not being as uncommon as one might expect, she was relieved that Opal's case didn't fit in that category. Now she only had to treat the injury, not an entire family situation.

"Did you black out?"

"No. The lights turned dim and my head hurt like the dickens, but I was fine. A little sick to my stomach maybe, but and's sake! My head didn't even bleed, so I don't know what all the fuss is about."

"Why didn't you tell your daughter what happened?"

"Because she's been after me to move into one of those assisted living homes. I tell you, it's a ridiculous idea." Opal's affront was obvious. "I'm perfectly able to care for myself and I already have a home. Why should I give it up?"

"Maybe she doesn't want you to be alone in case you have an accident."

Opal's faded brown eyes reflected worry. "You're not going to tell her, are you?"

"You need a CT scan, which is a fancy X-ray of your skull," Dixie explained. "Your daughter will want to know why."

"So would I. I'm still capable of making my own decisions," Opal said waspishly.

"Of course you are," Dixie soothed. "The scan will tell me if you damaged something inside your head. Your scalp didn't bleed, but your unsteadiness and trembling could be signs that you're bleeding inside your skull."

Opal's eyes widened, as if the idea fell completely out of the realm of possibility. "Are you sure?"

"No," Dixie said honestly, "which is why we need a scan to see what's going on."

"All right." She nodded, then closed her eyes. "This won't take long, will it? At four, I always watch my TV show."

If Dixie's suspicions were correct, Opal wouldn't watch the television for several days. "I'd plan on being at the hospital for a couple of hours."

"Hours? Well, I suppose I have nothing else to do." Opal's voice faded and she closed her eyes. "Suddenly, I don't feel very well…"

In the next instant she stiffened and her extremities began to jerk. At the same time she rigidly arched her back.

Dixie grabbed onto Opal to keep her from falling off the table. "She's having a seizure. Call 911, find an endotrach tube, oxygen, and page Dr Cameron, stat."

CHAPTER SEVEN

"AMBULANCE is on the way." Miranda hung up the phone and began rummaging through a cupboard.

"Fine, but where's my tube?" Dixie asked, trying to keep the older lady from literally jumping off the table. She was doing everything medically possible, given the circumstances, but knowing that didn't lessen her impatience over the lack of equipment and variety of drugs she was accustomed to having at her fingertips.

"Sorry. I only have an oropharyngeal airway." Miranda brandished it in the air.

"I'll take it." Actually, Dixie thought it might be more beneficial at the moment. Not only would the device allow them to mechanically ventilate Opal if necessary, it would also act as a bite block. Because she couldn't force it into Opal's mouth without potentially causing her to vomit or aspirate, Dixie waited for the right second to insert it.

"Come on, Opal," she urged. "Open wide."

When the right moment came, she slipped the airway between Opal's teeth and positioned it past her tongue.

Miranda handed her a blanket, and while Dixie covered their patient the nurse pulled a small cylinder of oxygen out of the cabinet. "Do you want me to set this up?"

"Yes."

Miranda spoke as she adjusted the valves on the oxygen tank. "Why is she having a seizure?"

"I think she has a subdural hematoma and it's putting pressure on her brain. I don't suppose we have any saline or lactated Ringer's to set up an IV line."

"Sorry. We did at one time, but it got outdated and the doctors decided not to replace it."

Dixie made a mental note to discuss that issue with Mark. "Do we have any diazepam?" she asked, referring to the drug that was a combination of fast-acting sedative, anticonvulsant and muscle relaxant.

"In the other room."

Dixie debated her options. The medication was best administered via IV, but since they didn't have IV access... No matter. If need be, she could get around it. "How long until the ambulance arrives?"

"A couple of minutes."

Minutes, thank goodness. "What about Dr Cameron?"

"I dialed his cellphone, but he didn't answer."

"Doesn't he carry a pager?"

"I tried that, too, but he doesn't usually carry both and he said to use his phone if we needed him. I'd better alert Jane so, if he calls, she'll know what to say."

"Tell her that if he hasn't answered in a couple of minutes, keep trying. Meanwhile, get the diazepam."

Miranda obeyed instantly. Dixie stayed at Opal's side to monitor her. She could do little else until the seizures stopped or the proper equipment arrived. As for Opal's flailing limbs, restraining her wasn't an option—Dixie could only make sure that the woman didn't hit anything or fall onto the floor.

She adjusted the blanket to keep it tucked around the elderly woman's petite form, although it was a somewhat futile effort. Maintaining Opal's body temperature was a small thing to do, but very necessary.

For the next several minutes Dixie impatiently watched both her patient and the clock. Just when she wondered if everyone had deserted her, the door opened and Mark strode in.

"Jane said we had a problem," he said without preamble.

"It's Opal Landers." Dixie explained the situation, finishing with, "The ambulance is on its way. Do you have a neurosurgeon in Hope?"

He shook his head. "We'll have to airlift her to another facility. How long has she been like this?"

Dixie glanced at the clock again. "Some minutes."

"Why wasn't I called?" Before Dixie could answer, he glanced around the room. "Where's Miranda?"

"In the med room. She'll be—"

Miranda rushed in, an ampule in her hand. "Got it."

Mark flashed his light in Opal's eyes. "Left pupil is fixed and dilated. She's not going to come out of this on her own. What are you waiting for? Draw up the diazepam."

"We were just getting ready to do that," Dixie said sharply, not appreciating Mark's attitude, "before we were so rudely interrupted."

She met his gaze across the exam table and raised one eyebrow. He didn't respond, except to hold out his hand for the syringe Miranda slapped in his palm.

"Hold her arm," he ordered.

All three of them held Opal's arm while Mark injected the drug directly into a large vein. When he spoke, his voice was even, but Dixie could sense his irritation.

"Why didn't anyone call me?"

"We tried," Miranda said defensively, "but—"

"But nothing. I shouldn't have to learn what's going on in my own practice as I walk in the door."

"She did try," Dixie said, adding her support to the nurse, who was clearly offended by his accusation.

"The recording said your phone wasn't switched on," Miranda added. "I tried your pager, too."

"I had other calls, so you must have dialed the wrong number."

"I don't know what to say," Miranda replied stiffly. "I tried." Her set jaw indicated that her patience had come to an end.

Dixie's own patience was hanging by a thread, but yelling at him in the middle of Opal's emergency wasn't appropriate or professional. When the time came, however, Dixie intended to be first in line to give him a piece of her mind.

Meanwhile, Opal needed their attention, not their bickering.

"Shouldn't the ambulance be here by now?" she asked impatiently.

As if on cue, the door opened and two paramedics strode in. Eager to get her hands on the equipment they carried, Dixie barely recognized Annie and Mic.

"This is becoming a habit," Annie said with a smile as she set her box at her feet.

"Tell me about it," Dixie replied, before she described the situation they'd just walked into. "The injection we gave her is taking effect, so start an IV with normal saline, not dextrose. I want the ER staff to be able to use phenytoin."

Annie nodded, as if aware of the incompatibility between that particular anticonvulsant drug and the sugar solution.

"She may seize again before you get back to the hospital, so give another dose of diazepam, IV push," Dixie ordered. "If you'll hand over an endotrach tube, I'll insert it."

By now Opal had lapsed into unconsciousness, so the group quickly started to work. Annie proficiently took care of the IV line, Mic monitored Opal's cardiac rhythms and vital signs and Dixie inserted the airway tube with Mark's assistance. Meanwhile, Mic called out the numbers, which, for the moment, weren't too bad. So far Opal was holding her own, but that could change in an instant.

Eager for Opal to be in the ER rather than their little examination room, Dixie announced, "Let's go, people."

Mark turned away from the wall phone. "I notified the ER. They'll run the scan as soon as you guys get there," he said to the paramedics, before he addressed Dixie. "Jared will call us when Radiology is finished."

They transferred Opal to the ambulance gurney. While Annie and Mic wheeled their patient toward the exit, Dixie nudged Mark. "How well do you know her daughter, Karen?"

"Well enough to know she'll be upset by the news." He paused. "Do you want me to talk to her?"

She was surprised that he'd asked. She'd almost expected him to take charge of that job, too. Yet he hadn't, so she decided to be magnanimous. "I'll do it, but she might be more comfortable if you came along. If you don't mind."

Their entourage had barely entered the hallway when Karen rushed forward. "What's wrong with my mother? Why the ambulance? How is she?"

"She's in a serious condition," Dixie explained as the paramedics disappeared from view. "She had a seizure, probably due to her head injury. I suspect she's bleeding inside her skull, but we won't know for certain until we look at her CT scan."

Karen stared at her, clearly puzzled. "A *head* injury? How? When?"

"She hit her head this morning on the silverware drawer."

"This morning? But...I was there the whole time. I didn't hear anything. She never said a word either."

"Apparently you were in another room at the time."

"And if the scan shows a problem, then what?"

Mark answered. "She'll need surgery. We'll make arrangements for a transfer to the nearest neurology unit."

Karen slumped against the wall. "When I saw her acting strange, slurring her words and acting weaker than usual, I thought age was just catching up with her. But this...it's absolutely bizarre. We've all knocked our heads on something or another."

"I wish I could explain the reasons why, but all it takes are the right conditions. The blood thinner she's on increased her risk."

Karen rubbed her face in obvious frustration. "I suppose, but I don't understand why she didn't tell me she'd hurt herself."

Dixie understood Karen's dismay. The woman had clearly been trying to do everything possible to look after her mother.

"For one thing, she thought that it was a minor bump—one of those things that happen and we simply forget it and go on. Then, as she started feeling poorly, she was afraid to tell you."

"But why?"

"She thought that if you knew, you'd push harder for her to move into another facility."

Karen's expression fell. "This is all my fault."

"No, it isn't," Mark answered. "Her injury was an accident. The damage was done and had nothing to do with you knowing about it or not."

"I could have brought her in sooner."

"Without any symptoms, we would have sent her home and asked you to watch her," Dixie pointed out. "Don't blame yourself. In the meantime, they'll take her to the hospital, run the scan, and then we'll decide what to do next."

Wearing her worry, Karen dashed off to alert her husband and meet him at the hospital.

Dixie watched the hallway empty. She'd done her job and placed Opal in capable hands. Jared Tremaine, as the ER physician, would arrange for Opal's transfer should it be necessary, so Dixie's responsibility had faded to consultant status for the family.

She faced Mark. "You didn't mention that I'd see so many ER cases."

"I would have warned you if I'd known myself. First a baby and now this. What's next?" His frustration was obvious in the way he rubbed the back of his neck.

"It could be worse," she assured him. "Shooting victims, stabbings and heart attacks come to mind. Look at it this way, our ER skills won't become rusty."

"No, they won't." He glanced around. "Where are your crutches?"

His question surprised her. "They're around here somewhere. Why?"

"Use them."

His dictatorial comment rankled. "In case you've forgotten, I'm a physician, too. I know my limits and when I decide that I need them, I'll use them. Not a minute before."

He opened his mouth to speak, then clamped his mouth shut.

Realizing she had the perfect lead-in for the heart-to-heart chat that Miranda had requested, she took advantage of the opportunity.

"I don't know what's the matter with—"

"Dr Albright?" Jane rounded the corner. "Could you work in an unscheduled patient? She's quite insistent about being seen today."

Eager to address her issues with Mark, she would have agreed to anything to keep from being interrupted. "Yeah, sure."

Before she could finish her earlier sentence, Jane added, "I put her in room two."

"I'll be right there."

Again, Jane paused. "If you don't see her now, we'll fall behind schedule worse than we have."

Mark answered, his temper clearly aroused. "She *said* she'd be—"

Dixie sighed inwardly and she laid a calming hand on his arm. "I'm coming, Jane."

Apparently satisfied by her answer, Jane disappeared, but not before she glowered at Mark.

"What is with everybody today?" he grumbled.

"I'd tell you, but it would take too long to explain. Duty calls, so I'll catch you later."

She headed toward room two where Miranda caught her. "Did you talk to him?" she asked in a whisper.

"Not yet. But I will. Before the day's over," Dixie tacked on.

"Don't forget," Miranda warned.

"I won't." After seeing his short temper about the phone and feeling its effects for herself, she understood why both women had been trying to blend into the woodwork when he was nearby. She, however, wouldn't endure his surliness indefinitely.

Her patient was a twenty-seven-year-old woman, Larissa Grayson. She was a long-haired brunette of medium height, and wore a colorful sweater vest with her jeans. She was also quite attractive, although it was obvious from the tension on her face and in her shoulders that something weighed heavily on her mind.

Her chart didn't show any record of medical problems and, other than an elevated systolic blood pressure reading, her vital signs were good. Nerves, Dixie decided.

She greeted her with a smile. "What can I do for you?"

"I'm pregnant," Larissa said flatly.

"Are you sure?"

"According to three kits from the drug store, I am. I haven't had a period either, since the first of December."

"Do you mind if I run a lab test of my own and examine you?"

"That's why I'm here. To be absolutely sure."

Dixie gave her a few minutes of privacy to collect a urine sample and undress for a pelvic exam. Even without Miranda's results of the pregnancy test, Dixie could tell from the cervical changes that Larissa was indeed pregnant.

Although Larissa answered Dixie's questions, she wasn't particularly forthcoming. Neither did she project the image of an excited mother-to-be.

"Does the father know?" Dixie asked, wondering if that was causing her patient to be upset.

"Yes." Larissa hesitated. "He's not very happy with me right now."

"It takes two," Dixie said practically, irritated that there were still men in the world who expected the woman to assume all responsibility for birth control.

"He knows. We just have a lot of other issues to work out."

"Is the baby one of them? If you're thinking about an abortion—"

"I'm not." Larissa's vehemence surprised Dixie. "No matter what happens, I want my child. *Our* child. I have a good job, so I can support myself and the baby, even if he won't."

Dixie patted her shoulder. "I'm glad to hear you've made your decision. As for you, continue your normal activities. Eat right, get plenty of rest, and take prenatal vitamins."

"When do I need to see you again?"

"We'll set up an appointment for you in a month, but I won't be here. You'll probably see Dr Cameron."

Larissa's face reflected her dismay. "I wanted you."

Dixie smiled. "Thanks for the vote of confidence, but I'm only filling in for a few weeks until Dr Cameron finds a couple of full-time physicians to bring on board."

Her face blanched. "He's looking for a couple of doctors? Isn't…won't Dr Bentley come back?"

Dixie wished she had the answer to that question. "I'm not sure," she hedged. "It depends on a number of things. If he's able to return, then perhaps you could see him, instead of Dr Cameron."

"Oh, no." Larissa shook her head. "No, I couldn't."

The faint blush on the woman's face gave away more than she probably realized, which set Dixie to wondering…

"Do you know Dr Bentley?" she asked.

Larissa grew even more wary. "Yes."

Dixie felt as if the puzzle piece she'd been waiting for had finally appeared. It took all her self-control to stop the questions from bubbling out of her.

"Professionally or personally?"

Once again, a pink hue flooded Larissa's face and she avoided Dixie's gaze. "I saw him a few times. Here, in the office." She rose. "Can I go now?"

"I'm finished," Dixie said, disappointed that she couldn't follow the best lead she'd stumbled across, "provided you'll agree to see someone other than Dr Bentley in a month. You want to give your baby the best prenatal care possible, don't you?"

"Yes, but…" Larissa furrowed her brow and played with her lower lip. "I suppose it will be OK to see Dr Cameron by then."

Her comment didn't make sense, unless she'd seen both men in a personal capacity. While Dixie didn't care if Larissa had dated Ned, the thought of Larissa and Mark being a couple didn't sit as well. "Excuse me?"

Larissa waved aside her comment. "Dr Cameron will be fine."

Dixie waited, hoping Larissa would explain further, but the other woman remained close-mouthed.

The room's intercom blared to life. "Dr Albright?" Miranda asked. "ER is on the line."

"Thanks. I'll pick up in a second," she called out. Lowering her voice to speak to Larissa, she said, "Then it's settled. We'll schedule you to see Dr Cameron in four weeks' time."

Larissa's face turned white. "You're Dr Albright?"

Once again, the woman's response surprised Dixie because she'd introduced herself when she'd first met her. "Yes."

"*Dixie* Albright?"

Dixie's mental antennae started to quiver. "Yes."

"Oh my gosh."

Clearly Larissa knew Ned far better than she claimed. No one in Hope knew Dixie at all, except for Ned, and he was gone. Playing a hunch, she asked, "Did Ned mention me?"

The girl looked like a deer caught in headlights—startled and unsure in which direction to turn. Then, just as quickly, she squared her shoulders and the surprise left her eyes.

"He may have. I don't remember. May I go now? I'm late for work."

The blinking light on the telephone's second line was a beacon, reminding Dixie of more important responsibilities than tracking down her cousin. Torn between dragging answers out of Larissa and dealing with Opal Landers and the ER, Dixie reluctantly let Larissa go.

"If you have any problems before your next appointment," she said as she crossed the space to reach the phone, "come back. Otherwise we'll see you in a month."

By the time Dixie picked up the receiver, Larissa had disappeared.

"Jared Tremaine here," the ER doctor said. "You were right. Opal Landers's CT scan shows a subdural hematoma.

I've made arrangements for a transfer. The helicopter should arrive in the next ten to fifteen minutes.''

''Thanks. How is she?''

''We've given meds to reduce the swelling in her brain and keep her seizures under control. She's stable from my standpoint, but the family would like to talk to you.''

''I'll be there in a few minutes.''

Having decided to throw caution to the wind and manage without her crutches today, Dixie limped to Jane's desk and discovered an empty reception area. Too impatient to find her or anyone else, she scribbled a terse note, jotted down her cellphone number and taped the scrap of paper to Jane's computer.

When she returned, she intended to find out everything she could about Larissa Grayson.

''Where *is* everybody?'' Mark groused as he strode down the hallway.

Miranda came out of another exam room. ''I'm here. Jane's in her office, and I have three people waiting to see you.''

''Where's Dix—er, Dr Albright?''

''In her rooms, I'd guess.''

''She isn't,'' he snapped. ''I checked.''

''Maybe she went to the ER. They called earlier. She must have left shortly after that.''

He didn't know why her absence bothered him, but it did. ''She should have told someone. I might have needed her. Did she take her crutches?''

''I saw them propped against her desk, so I assume not.''

''Fool woman,'' he muttered.

Jane ambled out of her office, papers in hand. ''Lab reports just came,'' she said cheerfully.

''Do you know where Dr Albright is?'' Mark asked as he took the pages she handed him.

''She went to ER. I taped her note to your door.''

He'd been too busy to set foot near his private office. He

craned his neck to peer down the hallway and caught a glimpse of something white tacked to the doorjamb.

"Can't we talk to people instead of leaving notes?" he grumbled. "It would be so much easier."

"But not necessarily safer," Miranda muttered.

He heard her remark, and was ready to respond in kind when he took a good look at his staff. Miranda wore a mulish expression, instead of her grandmotherly smile, and Jane looked like a scared rabbit, instead of the confident receptionist that she was.

Had two frustrating days turned him into such an ogre that even his staff were hard pressed to decide if they wanted to strangle him or run away? Or, in Dixie's case, both?

He drew a deep breath and forced himself to lower his voice a notch. "How many patients are left?"

"Three."

"Then let's finish so we can go home and start fresh in the morning."

He made short work of the last few cases, although, as he took out Robert Mullins's stitches in his arm, he realized that Dixie was supposed to have hers removed today, too.

Had she gone to Jared, or next door to the minor emergency center? As much as he liked the physicians who staffed those areas, jealousy attacked him with a vengeance. It didn't seem fair that she would ask one of *them* for help instead of asking him.

He couldn't blame her, he supposed. For the past two days he'd been acting like the grumpy man she'd accused him of being.

"OK, Robert," he said as he snipped the last stitch. "You're good as new."

"Thanks, Doc," the forty-five-year-old mechanic said.

"Stay clear of sharp metal parts next time."

"I will."

Several minutes later, after he'd handled the afternoon's most pressing details, he cornered Miranda. "I'm going to the hospital. Dr Albright may have run into a problem."

If the nurse thought his actions odd, she didn't comment. "Have a nice evening," she said instead.

He wanted it to be far more than "nice," but if simply spending the next few hours with Dixie was all that fate granted him, he'd take it and be satisfied. For now.

"I intend to."

At five-thirty, Dixie ambled through Hope City Hospital's corridors on her way downstairs from Peds. To the casual observer, she might appear as if she had all the time in the world, but nothing was further from the truth. Her knee ached, and because she hadn't brought her crutches with her during her mad dash to the ER she had to manage as best she could without them.

Her orthopedist might have encouraged her to lose the crutches today, but if he'd known that she would be conducting business as usual, he would have revised his recommendation.

Right now, all she longed for was a chance to elevate her leg and rest for an hour. It would mean that dinner for Mark would be delayed, but she didn't think he'd care. After the day they'd both had, he could use an hour to unwind, too.

What a day it had been! Fortunately, the medical helicopter had whisked Opal away to a neurosurgeon and should be arriving within the hour. Although the day had been filled with excitement and adrenalin-charged moments, the highlight had been meeting Larissa Grayson.

The woman knew Ned and knew him well. Dixie could hardly wait to talk to her again.

The emergency room loomed ahead and she ambled toward the double doors. Jared had agreed to remove her stitches if nothing major interfered. According to her watch, if he hurried, she could relax for a bit before she started dinner.

She pushed aside the thought of Mark volunteering for the task. Perhaps she should have asked him, but the sparks flying between them made her question if that would be an intelligent choice on her part. Jared was a far safer bet.

Inside the department, she found three men leaning against the counter in front of the nurses' station, appearing quite at ease in this now quiet department. Of the three, she only had eyes for the auburn-haired one who was chuckling over something.

She hadn't expected to see Mark until later tonight, but now that he was here she could hardly wait to tell him about Larissa.

Intent on her mission, she limped forward. "Hi, everyone," she said, recognizing Jared and Galen Stafford, the head of the minor emergency center.

Jared grinned. "Back so soon?"

"It doesn't take hours to make rounds when I only have one patient." She smiled at the men before she turned toward Mark and showed her excitement. "You'll never guess what I found out."

"Likewise," he answered, his smile vanishing as he transformed himself from the relaxed man she'd seen across the room to a serious, intense physician. "Is everything set up, Jared?"

"What's going on?" she asked, glancing from one man to the other.

"Room one is ready," Jared replied.

Mark took her arm. "Let's go."

"Wait a minute." She resisted his attempt to pull her along. "Go where?"

Jared shrugged apologetically. "Sorry to disappoint you, Dixie, but Annie just called from the fire station. She's cooking tonight and asked me to eat with the rest of her crew. Galen said he'd remove your stitches, but he has to leave, too. Mark said he didn't mind filling in for us."

She didn't consider herself a suspicious sort, but the situation screamed of being more than coincidence. "I see."

Mark raised one eyebrow. "Shall we?"

Wanting to refuse, she couldn't because the other two men watched her reaction with undisguised interest. "Oh, I guess," she said crossly. Little did Mark know that she didn't intend to let him near her leg. He'd find out soon enough after they lost their audience.

Conscious of Mark's light grip on her arm, she bided her time until they were alone inside the cubicle.

"If you think I'm going to let you touch me after you've been horrid all day," she began hotly, "you can think again."

"Horrid? I've been *horrid*?"

"Yes." She crossed her arms. "Miranda and Jane can't do anything to your satisfaction when I know that they're both experts in what they do. Personally, I don't appreciate having you watch over my shoulder either.

"As for you," she continued, unable to stop now that she'd started, "if you're taking grumpy pills, then you can dispose of them right now. Nobody wants to work with a guy who growls for no good reason. I understand your frustration. I have my own to deal with, but I'm not taking it out on everyone else."

He advanced until they stood toe to toe. His breath brushed across her cheek and her heart flip-flopped in her chest at his nearness.

The smoldering fire in his eyes seemed incongruous with his mild tone. "If we're both frustrated and I suspect it's for the same reason, then we only have one solution."

Her mouth went dry. "Which is?"

"To deal with it together."

Before she realized what was happening, he pulled her close and covered her mouth with his.

CHAPTER EIGHT

GOOD sense told Dixie to object. Who wanted to kiss a man who deserved a thorough dressing-down for acting like a jerk?

Heaven help her, but she did.

Vaguely conscious of their surroundings and aware they could be interrupted at any time, Mark's kiss seemed to last for ever, but she didn't care. The door was closed, the department quiet, and she wouldn't be surprised if Jared was standing guard outside.

He finally tore his mouth away. "I have been wanting to do that for the past two days," he said hoarsely.

She stared into gray eyes that reflected clear, calm skies instead of the gathering storm she'd seen earlier. "You have?"

"You don't know how hard it's been to look and not touch," he admitted. "Being noble isn't all it's cracked up to be."

"So if I tell you that we can't do this...?" She stood on tiptoe, brushed his cheek with her lips, then raised one eyebrow. "You'll—"

"If you think I'm short-tempered now, check again in a few days," he said wryly.

She fingered the second button on his shirt. "Miranda and Jane would commit murder and mayhem before then."

He lowered both arms to loosely encircle her waist and shifted her so that her hips nestled against his. "Then what happens next? It's obvious we can't ignore what's between us."

"Not if we want to keep a nurse and a receptionist," she agreed.

His eyes darkened. "What are you saying?"

She'd thought about this for the past two nights and had decided that if the opportunity arose again, she'd take it. As he'd said, life was too short and too precarious to play it safe. Why not enjoy each day as it came, including the pleasures it might hold?

However, now that she stood on the threshold of the opening she'd wanted, she hesitated. "I don't want to make a mistake," she said simply.

"Who said we'd be making one?"

"Things are moving so fast. What if—?"

"What if you stop thinking 'What if?'" he said. "Your 'what ifs' may never happen, and you'll have wasted all this time and energy."

"We're supposed to think in terms of 'what if,'" she reminded him. "That's how we were trained. If this happens, then you do that and if that happens, then you do something else."

"Can't we just take each day as it comes? Isn't that also what we're trained to do? We can be aware of all the possibilities and avoid as many as we can, but the truth is, we can't deal with a single one until it becomes reality."

He stroked her jawline. "The reality is this thing between you and me."

"What about Ned?"

"Won't you trust me to handle the situation in my own way?"

Placing Ned's future in someone else's hands was difficult at best. She'd spent nearly her entire life looking after him. Trusting someone else, giving up her role as mediator, wouldn't be easy, but if she didn't make the attempt, she was setting herself up to be Ned's crutch for the rest of his life, just as Mark had pointed out.

"I'll try," she said slowly. "I'll try to take one day at a time and I'll try to trust you to do the right thing where Ned is concerned."

"Good girl," he said, sounding pleased. "Now, take off your skirt."

Startled by his request, she leaned back as far as she could. "What?" she screeched.

He grinned as he helped her sit on the bed. "Time to remove your stitches. I'm hungry and I've been waiting for your famous enchiladas all day."

"Dinner will be late," she warned.

"Too bad. I'll eat dessert first."

"Dessert?" Oh, dear, she'd forgotten all about the last course.

He leaned over her. "This," he said, brushing a swift kiss across her lips, "is dessert. It's as addictive as chocolate."

She laughed. "Flattery will get you nowhere. My skirt stays right where it is."

"Spoilsport."

"Isn't this against the rules of doctor-patient relationships?"

"What?"

"Kissing the patient."

He grinned as he tugged on his latex gloves. "Rules are made to be broken. Besides, you're not my patient."

"From where I'm sitting, I am," she said as she raised her skirt to expose her knee and unstrap the brace.

"You're not," he assured her. "You're a colleague who's asked another for a favor."

"Speaking of favors, did Jared and Galen really have other commitments?"

"No."

"Thanks," she said dryly. "How am I ever going to face them again?"

"They needed a little help, too, to end up as happily married as they both are. I might add, however, that if you'd let me handle this in our office, neither one would have ever known."

"Ah. So this is my fault."

His expression was full of innocence. "Yeah."

"I beg to differ." She watched as he pulled the tray of supplies, which someone had thoughtfully laid out, closer to her, guided a wheeled stool beside the bed with his foot, then sat down.

"Do you want to watch or not?" he asked.

"I'll watch."

He grinned as he raised the head of the bed by pushing the buttons on the control panel. "Are you sure?"

"Positive. Watching someone work on me is different than doing it myself." She grinned. "And don't ask why I feel that way. A character flaw, I guess."

"If that's the worst flaw you have, you're downright perfect." He bent over her to examine the site.

Dixie didn't know why she suddenly felt so exposed. He was only looking at her leg, for Pete's sake. If he saw her in her jogging shorts, he'd see far more skin than he did now.

When he touched her knee, she jumped. "Sorry," she said, fighting the heat that rushed across her face.

"Are you sure you want to watch?"

If he thought her reaction was due to the upcoming procedure and not the mere brush of his hand across her skin, she refused to correct his faulty impression. "Absolutely."

She steeled herself to what would come next and focused on the back of his head as he started to work. He needed a haircut, she decided. Although tempted to run her hands along the column of his neck, she didn't. Startling him while he held a pair of scissors wasn't a good idea.

His motions were careful and controlled, and she gradually relaxed. Soon she was mesmerized by the sight of his long, lean fingers snipping threads and pulling them free.

This time, when he felt along the ridges and hollows of her knee, she didn't jump like a frightened rabbit. Instead, she enjoyed the view of his hands as he probed and prodded very carefully.

"No swelling. That's good," he said. "I don't think your surgeon expected you to stand on your feet all day, though."

She grinned. "What he doesn't know won't hurt him."

"I'm not worried about his injuries. Only yours."

A warm glow spread inside her. She sensed that Mark's

solicitude went beyond the usual regard a doctor held for his patient or another colleague. "Are you really? Worried, that is?"

"Concerned," he corrected. "Not worried."

"Thank you," she said simply.

Mark wondered why she sounded so appreciative of his interest in her well-being.

"Did your family hover over you when you had surgery?" he asked as he stripped off his gloves and cleared away the evidence of his handiwork.

She shrugged. "My aunt sent a get-well card."

All she'd received had been a card? Granted, her surgery hadn't been life-threatening, but a card? No flowers or, better yet, a personal visit? What kind of family did Dixie have? Last summer, after his plane crash, his parents and siblings had descended like a flock of locusts and he'd only suffered a broken collar-bone and gashes along his jaw and eyebrow. When they'd left a week later, he'd had enough flowers in his house to stock a floral shop, had received enough greeting cards to paper an entire wall, and had enough food in his freezer to last until Christmas.

"What about Ned?" He suspected the gist of her answer but had to ask anyway.

"I never told him. I tried calling, but he disappeared about that time, remember? It wouldn't have mattered anyway. Ours isn't a demonstrative family."

He thought of his boisterous clan. Hugs, impromptu visits and regular phone calls were the norm.

"Mine is," he said.

"You're lucky. That was the hardest adjustment for me when I moved in with my aunt and uncle. My parents were very loving, so it took me a while to get used to a different way of life."

The wistfulness in Dixie's voice tugged at him. If Ned ever showed his face around here again, Mark would give him a painful lesson on how to treat her. The more he learned about her relatives, the more he disliked them.

"When I have a family, I'll always have plenty of hugs and kisses for my husband and children," she finished vehemently.

He thought of what it would be like to come home each night if she were waiting at the door. A welcome kiss as soon as he crossed the threshold, an exuberant hug and a smile, and later, after they'd tucked Junior and Juniorette into bed, a long night spent entwined in each other's arms.

He'd drawn his mental picture vividly enough to send his blood raging through his body, which wasn't a good thing to do at the moment.

"He'll be a lucky man," he said. Then, because if they stayed in this cubicle for a moment longer, he might embarrass them both if they were caught, he held out his hand to help her stand. "We'd probably better let someone else have the room."

"We should." She slid her long skirt over her leg and took his hand. Mark swallowed his disappointment over the loss of such a delectable view. With legs like hers—slim, athletic, and long enough to wrap around a man's waist—it was a rotten shame to hide them. On the other hand, he'd bet that once summer rolled around, she'd turn men's heads without even trying.

The idea irritated him.

She glanced at her watch. "That didn't take long at all."

"Of course not. A few snips don't." Actually, they'd been holed up for at least thirty minutes—far longer than necessary for those same snips he'd mentioned, but he didn't think it necessary to bring that to her attention. She'd only be more embarrassed if they ran into Jared outside. While Mark wouldn't mind watching her skin turning a becoming shade of pink, she probably wouldn't appreciate seeing Jared's satisfied smirk or amused wink.

"Come on," he said. "I'll take you to dinner."

"I'm cooking, remember?"

"It's late. You've had a busy day."

"Be still, my heart," she said, crossing her hands over her

chest. "A man who accepts that a woman who works all day might be too exhausted to slave over a hot stove… I may faint from the shock of finding such a paragon."

"You have my mother to thank. And my sisters."

"They must be remarkable women."

"They are," he said. "One's a doctor and one's a nurse, so I can't claim that I have more stress and work harder than they do."

"Thanks for the thought and the invitation, but I've already planned dinner. It might be an hour late, but it won't be difficult to prepare."

"If you're certain."

"I am. Unless you've changed your mind about Mexican food?"

He didn't care what she served. Her cooking abilities were a boon, an unexpected pleasure, but not his main draw. *She* was.

"Not a chance."

Because Dixie had washed most of the dishes while the enchiladas baked in the oven, as soon as they finished eating, they only had to stack their plates in the dishwasher. Afterwards, Dixie led the way to the living room where they could enjoy the hot chocolate that Mark had requested.

"I'm not sure how well hot chocolate follows spicy Mexican food as an after-dinner drink," she warned as he accepted the mug she handed him.

"Your hot chocolate tastes good, which is all that matters."

She sank onto the couch beside him. "Thanks."

He patted his trim stomach. "I don't suppose you'll share the secret to your enchiladas."

"You helped fill them," she pointed out. "Did you see a jar labeled 'Secret Ingredient' on the counter?"

"No, but you didn't measure anything either. A sprinkle of this and a handful of that aren't good instructions."

She smiled. "What can I say? That's how I was taught."

"But my sprinkles and handfuls are bigger than yours."

As if she needed to be reminded how large his hands were…and how they felt.

"You realize you'll have to fill my freezer before you leave town."

"They're better if they're fresh. You'll have to drive to Chicago when your craving kicks in."

"I'll do that," he said.

He sounded quite serious. She wanted to believe him, but caution demanded otherwise. If she expected him to make the trek and then, for whatever reason, he didn't, she'd be crushed. It would be far better to take his comment in the teasing spirit in which it had probably been intended.

"You don't think I will, do you?" he asked.

The light-hearted atmosphere had suddenly shifted in the opposite direction. She couldn't lie to him. "No."

"Why not?"

"For one thing, you'll be busy," she said bluntly. "Busy with breaking in your new partners or busy with patients if you don't fill your positions. You may want to visit, but we both know that personal plans fall by the wayside when there aren't enough hours in the day."

He leaned forward and cupped his mug in both hands. "If I say I'll meet you in Chicago or anywhere in between, I will."

"Do you always follow through on your plans?"

"If they're important, yes."

She wanted to ask if she fell into his "important" category, but didn't. She wasn't ready to hear his answer, whatever it might be.

"Is someone special waiting for you at home?" he asked.

"You mean, other than my landlord and the colleagues who are covering my shifts? No." His mention of someone special triggered her memory and she scooted to the edge of her seat.

"Oh my gosh, I just remembered what I wanted to tell you when I saw you in the ER. I can't believe it slipped my mind."

He interrupted with a feral smile. "I can. You did have another person demanding your attention."

She smiled at his obvious reference to himself. All things considered, it was a wonder she remembered her own name. "I know, but this is so fantastic, you aren't going to believe it."

"I'm all ears."

She set her mug on the table, certain she'd spill it in her excitement. "Right after we had the incident with Opal, I saw a young lady by the name of Larissa Grayson in the office. I think she knows Ned."

"Lots of people know Ned."

"Yes, but I think she knows Ned better than most. For one thing, when I mentioned that she'd need to see either you or one of the physicians you hired at her next appointment, she asked if Ned would be coming back."

"Everyone has asked the same question," he said dryly.

"Yes, but when I said that he might and if so, we could schedule her to see him, she was adamantly opposed to the idea."

"Maybe she met him and didn't like him or his bedside manner. It happens."

"I thought of that, but when Miranda mentioned my name on the intercom, Larissa turned pale." Dixie scooted closer. "She *knew* me, Mark. She'd said that Ned had mentioned my name. Now, if no one else in town, including yourself, knew who I was, then those two have to be more than casual acquaintances."

"Maybe. Maybe not. They might have talked about their families at some point."

"Do *you* remember the names of your patients' relatives?"

"No."

"I rest my case."

"If you're right and she knows Ned personally, then what?"

"She's pregnant." Before he could interrupt, she rushed on. "I wondered if she might be Ned's former girlfriend—

the one who was supposed to attend the Christmas party with him and didn't. It might explain why she didn't want to see you.''

''Ned never mentioned a Larissa Grayson,'' Mark said. ''He called his girlfriend June.''

''Are you sure?''

''Absolutely. I distinctly remember him referring to her as 'his little June bug.' ''

Undaunted, she pressed on. ''Maybe she goes by her middle name. What did she look like?''

''I only saw her once. Tall, I think. Light brown hair, medium length. Glasses, too.''

Larissa was tall, but she had short dark hair and no glasses. But any hairdresser and a set of contacts could account for those minor changes.

''It might be the same girl. I think we should check her out.''

''How do you suggest we start?''

''She claims she's seen Ned in the office, so I'm sure we'll have her address and phone number in our files. Once I have that information, I'll pay her a visit.''

''It's worth a try, but wait until Saturday. I'll go with you.''

His offer was totally unexpected and extremely welcome. ''You really want to come along?''

''Yeah. Why not?''

''All right. It's a date.'' Without thinking, Dixie scooted closer, leaned against him and flung her arms around his neck. ''Thank you.''

His hands rested on her back and held her firmly in place as he met her gaze. ''You're welcome.''

Suddenly, her position registered on her brain. Filled with mortification by her impulsive action, she wanted to move away and found that she couldn't. Not only did her entire body ignore her mental commands to crawl out of his lap, but his hold didn't lessen either.

His gaze traveled to her mouth and she knew what he wanted. Because she wanted to taste him again, she parted her lips ever so slightly in anticipation. His breath brushed across the bridge of her nose, and she felt his chest heave underneath her palm.

"I hope this isn't the way you thank everyone," he said in a lazy drawl.

"It isn't," she assured him.

"Good." He lowered his head, but as his mouth touched hers, her phone rang. "Damn," he mumbled.

Her sentiments, exactly.

Dixie scrambled for the nearest unit, which was in the kitchen. She listened to the man on the other end and then returned to the living room with a light step.

"That was the ER. A Hal Owens. Do you know him?" she asked.

"We have a contract with an agency to staff our ER. He's one of the docs who sometimes covers."

"Ah. Anyway, he received word about Opal Landers. Apparently she made it through surgery and is stable."

"That's great."

"The neurosurgeon says she'll need a long period of rehab. She may never regain a complete recovery, but over time and without further complications she should come close."

"Her family will be relieved to hear that."

"What's bad is that Opal may end up in some sort of assisted living complex," she said darkly. "She'll be so disappointed."

"She's a smart woman. Once she comes to terms with her limitations, she may agree it's the best place for her." He rose and held out his arms. "Now, where were we?"

She stepped into his embrace. "Right here, I believe."

Before Mark could pull her close, his cellphone jingled a jaunty tune. "What now?" he growled before he barked his name at the person who'd dared to interrupt.

A fraction of a second later, his body tensed.

"Who?" he asked, then shook his head at the apparent answer. "I'll be right there."

"What's wrong?"

He clipped the phone back on his belt. "The police caught a couple of kids shooting out windows with BB guns."

"Your house?"

"The clinic," he corrected. "I need to go."

"Did they catch them?"

"In the act. Unfortunately one of the boys is Robbie Whittaker. Walt's son."

He spoke as if she should know who Walt was. "Do I know him?"

"Walt was the physician who was killed in our plane crash. He'd invited a couple of us to his friend's cabin in the Ozarks. He flew Jared, myself, and Justin St James down there for a mini-vacation."

"And Robbie?"

"The boy hasn't adjusted to or accepted his dad's death. It seems that he targets the medical establishment," he finished dryly.

"Then you aren't the only one who lost a few windows?"

"Justin did, too." He planted a hard kiss on her mouth. "Gotta run."

"I'm coming along." She hurried to the coat closet to grab her wrap, as well as his.

"It's cold and it's late…" he began.

She shrugged on her coat and tugged on her gloves. "And you're wasting time."

The scene at Mark's building wasn't as bad as Dixie had expected. Two police cars with their lights flashing were parked in front. Several officers were tramping over the ground as they shone flashlights across Mark's windows and those in the building next door.

As soon as Mark and Dixie slid out of the car, an officer who'd been assessing the building approached them. "Dr Cameron?"

"Yes?"

"As near as we can tell, three windows are busted. Apparently the boys decided to have a little target practice."

"Target practice?"

Dixie followed the two men as they headed toward the large picture windows that were in Jane's office and the waiting area.

"They drew circles on the glass and tried to hit the centers," the officer explained. "The glass is still intact, other than the BB holes, so you shouldn't need to board up the windows. A strip of duct tape should hold things together until morning."

Dixie moved in close to eye the small holes. The damage was beyond a patch job; the windows would need to be replaced. Remembering how a friend of hers who'd replaced a picture window had complained of the cost, she multiplied the figure by three and winced. This was definitely an expense that Mark didn't need or could afford at this time.

"And you're certain it was Robbie Whittaker?" Mark asked.

The officer shrugged. "He claims he didn't shoot the guns, but the other boys deny using them, too. We'll let the detectives sort out the truth. Even if Robbie was a bystander, he was at the scene, which doesn't look good for his innocence."

Mark nodded. "I understand."

"We'll file our report so you can notify your insurance company first thing in the morning," the policeman told him. "In the meantime, we'd like you to walk through and look for other damage."

"I will."

The officer moved away to confer with his colleagues and left Mark and Dixie gazing at the windows. She placed a hand on his arm.

"I know it's bad, but it's only a few panes of glass."

"Yeah, only glass," he echoed. "We'd better check inside."

Shards of glass lay on the carpeting and sparkled like diamonds under the overhead lights. Other than a broken vase that a stray BB pellet had hit, the rooms were untouched.

"It won't take long to whip things back into shape," she told him as he rummaged through Jane's desk drawer to find a roll of gray tape. "I'll help as soon as the insurance company sends someone to look things over."

"You'll be waiting a long time."

The flat note in his voice gave her pause. "What? Don't you have insurance?"

"I do, but I changed my policy to one with a higher deductible. Even if I file a claim, I'll still have to pay most of the cost."

Dixie didn't need to ask what had prompted him to change his policy or when. He'd probably done so after Ned had cleared out the practice's bank account. She started to say that he didn't need to worry about the money when he continued.

"At least they used a pellet gun instead of throwing rocks," he said. "We can manage for a while without replacing the windows."

"You don't need—" she began.

The door burst open and a woman about Dixie's age poked her head inside Jane's inner sanctum. "Mark?" she asked.

Dixie swallowed the rest of her statement. She'd tell him later that he didn't need to worry about the cost.

"Julia," he responded with a smile. "You shouldn't have come down here."

"I had to," she said simply. Her eyes were red-rimmed and her short blond hair was tousled, as if she'd run her hands through it repeatedly in the last hour. "I can't tell you how sorry I am."

"It's not your fault," Mark told her.

"Robbie was doing so well. The therapist said so just the other day. And now this."

"He had a setback. That's all." He patted her shoulder.

"Did he?" she asked, her voice dull. "Or are we continuing a pattern that we can't escape?"

"He's a good kid. Confused right now, but give him time. He'll come around."

Julia wiped the moisture off her cheeks and nodded. "I hope so. He said he didn't do it, but…" She cleared her throat.

"But he was involved," he said gently. "He has to pay the consequences."

Julia sniffled. "I know."

"I'll expect Robbie to mow the lawn all summer, both here and at my house, as restitution."

"I'll tell him."

Dixie frowned. She wanted to interrupt and ask how many years it would take Robbie to pay him back. Mark might not be able to afford the window, but to lay such a huge debt on a teenager was completely ridiculous. Where was his compassion? His mercy?

He didn't have any, she railed inside. And if he didn't have any for a thirteen- or fourteen-year-old boy, she couldn't expect him to show any for a thirty-year-old.

And yet, as Dixie watched the two interact she noticed how Mark readily gave Julia Whittaker the moral support she needed. Within minutes the other woman seemed less beaten down, and a smile, albeit a weak one, occasionally crossed her face.

Finally, Julia hugged him and stepped away. "Thanks for everything, Mark," she said clearly. "Let's hope that spending his summer behind a lawnmower will teach him how to be responsible for his actions."

Her comment caught Dixie off guard, and yet the more she thought about it she realized that Mark wasn't uncompassionate or unmerciful. He could have handed Robbie the crutch of sympathy because he was having trouble dealing with the death of his father, but he didn't. Instead, he was using his own brand of tough love so that Robbie would grow up to be a trustworthy, dependable individual.

Mark was truly an unusual man to be that concerned over a young boy, and after realizing just how unusual he was she also realized that she was a breath away from falling in love with him.

No, she wasn't that far away. She was falling right now, head over heels.

For the first time since she'd promised to trust him to do

the right thing with Ned, she honestly believed that he would. If only she'd learned her lesson before she'd called her bank and arranged a transfer of funds shortly after she'd learned of Ned's sticky fingers.

She had to tell Mark what she'd done and hope that he'd accept her explanation and apology, because hurting him was the last thing she wanted to do.

CHAPTER NINE

FRIDAY morning, Dixie peered over Jane's shoulder at her computer screen. "What do you mean, you don't have a record for Larissa Grayson?"

"Just that," Jane replied. "Yesterday was her first visit."

"But she told me she'd been here before."

"If she came through those doors, I'd have a file on her on my computer," Jane insisted. "Unless Dr Bentley saw her after hours or off the record."

"Which means that she might be more than just a regular patient," Dixie mused aloud, excited that she could be on the right track.

"If that's what happened then, yes, I'd agree."

Mark strolled in. "Who might be more than a regular patient?"

"We think Larissa Grayson is," Jane explained.

"You don't think you're adding two plus two and ending up with five?" he asked.

"We might," Dixie admitted, "but once we talk to her again, preferably not here, we'll know for sure." She pointed to the computer screen. "What's her address from yesterday's entry?"

"Hang on. The computer's slow today for some reason." After a few keystrokes, Jane read the information. "She listed a post office box."

"A post office box?" The news couldn't have been more disheartening. "What about a phone number?"

"None."

"Her employer?"

Jane shook her head. "Blank."

Dixie slumped in a chair. "I can't believe we hit another dead end."

"Ned covered his tracks," Mark said, sounding unsurprised. "As I said before—"

"We won't find him until he wants to be found. I know." Dixie squared her shoulders, pasted a smile on her face, and rose. "Well, so much for that lead. Thanks for checking, Jane."

"My pleasure."

Mark watched Dixie disappear down the hall. Although she'd put on a good front, he could tell this latest roadblock had effectively dampened her spirits.

"She's really upset, isn't she?" Miranda asked.

He nodded.

"You know, for all Ned's faults, he was a nice guy," Jane interjected. "The patients seemed to like him."

"So did the nurses," Miranda said dryly. "Or so I heard."

"I know he tended to disappear without warning," Jane went on, "but it's hard to believe he'd walk away from everything he owns without a word. Not just to us, but to his family." She shook her head.

"I feel sorry for Dixie, but what can we do?" Miranda asked.

Jane looked thoughtful. "Maybe we should hire a private investigator."

"With what?" Mark asked wryly. Ned had already helped himself to twenty thousand dollars. Spending money to find him seemed like a total waste of his limited resources. "Don't forget, we have windows to replace, too."

Miranda straightened from her perch on Jane's desk. "As much as I hate to mention finances, I'll be happy to float the practice a loan so Jane won't go buggy looking at the gray tape on the windows."

Jane scoffed. "Who has time to look out of the windows? But count me in, too."

Mark smiled. No matter how many times he might grouse about his help, they were both worth more than he could ever pay them. "Thanks. I appreciate the offer, but we aren't in completely dire straits. We did get a bank loan, remember?"

"True," Jane admitted. "But you only borrowed a fraction of what Ned took, which means that we're skating close to our bottom line. If anything else happens…"

"Then we'll deal with it." Mark flashed each one a wide grin to soften his next statement. "Meanwhile, you should both be doing something to earn your generously high salaries."

Jane hooted and Miranda snorted at his exaggeration, but he'd accomplished his goal of letting them know he wasn't worried about his financial situation and neither should they.

OK, maybe he *was* worried, a little. Who wouldn't be? Yet he had enough faith in himself and his staff to know they'd weather this particular storm.

Mark headed down the hall, then stopped outside Dixie's office. It was obvious when she'd left Jane's cubicle that she needed a boost to her spirits, and he had a good idea what might work.

Before he could poke his head inside, he heard her side of a conversation.

"No, Aunt Cora. I haven't been able to find him.

"Yes, I've tried.

"He could be anywhere.

"I know he's my cousin, but—

"I know you're upset, but I—

"Yes, I'll call you again in a couple of days.

"No matter what, I'll call. Bye."

She hung up the phone and pinched the bridge of her nose in obvious frustration.

Mark ambled in. "I couldn't help but overhear. Your aunt?"

Dixie nodded. "I didn't get a chance to mention the stolen money."

"Tell her next time. Or call her back now."

"She doesn't think I'm putting in enough effort to find him, so I'd rather wait a few days to hear the second verse of the same song,'' she confessed.

"You're a doctor, not a missing persons expert."

"I know, but I still feel like I'm failing."

"You're doing everything you possibly can, aren't you?"

"I think so, but she—"

"Don't worry what she thinks. If you want my opinion, cut yourself some slack. To help you do that, I have the perfect plan."

She smiled. "You do?"

"A night on the town. We'll go to dinner, then to a movie, maybe even a little bowling, if you're up to it."

"You're on call, though."

"I'm *always* on call," he informed her. "If I let that stop me, I'd never leave my house."

Dixie tugged on her lower lip as if considering his offer. "I don't know... I'm not really in the mood. I should visit the neighbors and—"

"The best way to find your mystery Ms Grayson is to appear in public. Hope isn't big enough to avoid people indefinitely. We might run into her at the grocery store, a restaurant, or the movie theater. Staying at home only limits your opportunities."

Her smile slowly grew to sunshiny proportions, as if she'd needed to give herself permission to enjoy herself. "OK. You're on."

"Great. I'll pick you up at six-thirty. You have until then to decide on a plan for the evening."

"If we attempt everything you mentioned, it'll be a long night," she warned.

"No one said we have to squeeze everything into our schedule at once. Tomorrow's another day." She didn't realize it, yet, but Mark intended to spend as much of the weekend with her as he possibly could.

"How's the Jamison baby doing?" Mark asked as they left the crowded seafood restaurant that evening after dinner.

Everyone in town must have suffered from cabin fever because all the eating establishments were packed and they'd waited nearly an hour for a table.

Yet she didn't mind. They'd passed the time in the bar, drinking soda. He'd offered to order a glass of wine for her, but simply being with Mark gave her enough of a high that she refused. Afterwards she'd eaten a delicious dinner of scampi while he'd dined on crab legs. Although it had been dark for hours, at nine o'clock the night was technically still young.

"He's doing much better. If he keeps making progress, I'll probably send him home on Monday."

"Have his cotinine results come back yet?"

"No, but I'm hoping to have the numbers before I discharge him. If not, I'll come up with plan B."

"It's going to be hard to catch the father," he warned. "And he's the one you need to talk to."

"It would be easier if I could force the issue while Joey is still in the hospital, but if not, I'll think of another way." She slipped into the passenger seat before he gallantly closed the door behind her.

As soon as he slid into the driver's seat, she asked, "Is the bowling alley next?"

"Can your knee handle all that bending?"

"It's felt a lot better since you took out the stitches so unless you're planning a marathon, I think I can manage a frame or two," she said dryly.

"OK, but if you have any problems…"

"I'll let you know," she promised.

"You're in for a treat," he said as he drove across town "Friday night is Cosmic Bowling."

"Cosmic Bowling?"

"They shut off the house lights and use a lot of disco-type strobe lighting, along with black lights and, of course, plenty of loud music. The kids love it." He grinned. "Most of the time you can't see your mark on the floor, but that's what's fun."

"As long as you don't care if your partner gutters the ball," she said. "I haven't bowled in years."

"Don't worry. It's like riding a bike. It'll come back. And I'm not a great bowler either, so don't worry."

When he guided her toward the locker containing his personal bowling ball, she said, "I think I've been hustled."

"I used to play on a league team, but I dropped out last fall. Not enough time and it was hell trying to find a sub at the last minute. Now I just play for fun. Which is what we're going to have," he assured her as he steered her to their assigned lane. "Trust me."

She had more than fun, she had the time of her life. It took her half a game to fall back into the familiar step-and-glide stroll down the approach, although she modified her delivery to minimize how much she bent her knee. Eventually she developed a rhythm, stopped throwing gutter balls and started taking down a respectable number of pins.

Her opening score of seventy-five was quite disappointing and she vowed to do better. To her disappointment, the second game seemed destined to be a repeat of the first because her ball consistently veered away from the remaining pins so that she never could pick up her spares.

Mark, on the other hand, had no such problems. His ball curved in whichever direction he wanted.

"How do you *do* that?" she complained good-naturedly.

His lopsided smile made him seem years younger. "A little bit of practice and a lot of luck."

"Somehow, I think it's the opposite. This time I'm going to watch your every move."

Her plan was a good one. As he stepped onto the approach, Dixie watched his stance, observing the easy way he held the ball. Then, as he moved forward, swinging his arm, her interest veered away from his bowling form to his bodily form.

He was a picture of harnessed power as he strode down the approach. His swing appeared relaxed, but his biceps and triceps bulged with effort. She'd noticed his broad shoulders and the play of muscles under his shirt before, but she hadn't taken the liberty of feasting her eyes on him as she was doing now.

His hair curled ever so slightly at his nape and she remembered how soft it felt, just as she remembered how it felt to have his arms around her.

Vaguely, she heard the ball crash into the pins and knew from the sound that none would have dared to remain standing. Instead of seeing for herself, she watched him turn toward her with a wide grin on his face. Under the brilliance of his smile, nothing else mattered.

"Did you see that?" he crowed. "A turkey. Three strikes in a row."

"Wow," she said, although she wasn't speaking about his score.

"Your turn."

"Why don't you finish my frames and I'll just watch?"

A worried wrinkle spread across his brow. "Did you overdo it?"

"Not at all. My knee feels great. I'm having plenty of fun."

His eyes took on a feral gleam. "In that case, you watched me. Now it's my turn."

Oh, dear.

"You'll tell me what I'm doing wrong?" she asked, rising.

"Absolutely."

Aware of his gaze following her every move, she tried her best to handle the ball with the same finesse that he did. While her ball did roll over the third arrow, it took a strange curve in front of the pins and only knocked down a couple.

She turned back to face him. "Well?" she demanded.

"Perfect," he murmured, his expression hungry enough to make her suspect he wasn't referring to her bowling prowess.

"Hardly," she said as she stood by the ball return.

"You just need to work on your follow-through."

Relieved that he *had* been watching her technique, she asked, "How do I do that?"

"I'll show you." He pulled her away from the equipment and stood behind her, spoon fashion. With him so close, she could hardly breathe, much less pay attention to her lesson, but she forced herself to concentrate on his instructions. The inherent noise of the alley faded into the background as he spoke in her ear and grabbed her right wrist in his hand.

"Pull back," he said as he swung her arm like a pendulum. "Then, when it passes your body to the front…" again he demonstrated "…release the ball. Let your hand continue swinging, but hold it straight, like you're going to grab the center pin by the throat."

She gulped. Her own throat felt as dry as the Sahara.

"Try again."

Dixie didn't question her instructor. By the time he deemed her ready to try his technique on her own with an actual ball, his scent and rock-hard body were indelibly etched on her brain.

This time the ball didn't curve as much and she picked up her spare. Giddy with success, she hurried back to Mark. "I got 'em," she yelled, then reached up and impulsively kissed him.

Mark knew she'd done so without thinking, but after watching the sweet curve of her bottom as she threw her ball down the alley, he was primed and ready for more than a mere high-five for a job well done.

Just as quickly, he grabbed her by the waist and held her. "Remember that lesson for the next time."

Remember? What was he talking about? Even if she didn't, he'd never forget the feel of her nestled against him as he'd guided her arm through the proper motions.

For the next several frames, each time she made a spare or he made a strike he kissed her. Oh, he'd made it seem light-hearted and quite innocent, but by the end of the game he wasn't interested in bowling and it was obvious that she wasn't either.

"I'm thirsty," he said. "How about you?"

She glanced at the row of empty soda cans on their table. "You surely don't want more soda."

"I have something else in mind."

"Iced tea? Water?"

He shook his head and flashed the pleading look that his mother claimed she never could resist. "Hot chocolate."

She laughed. "OK. Let's go. Your place or mine?"

"I don't have the ingredients in my cupboard," he reminded her. "Whatever they are."

"Mine it is."

Once they arrived at her place, he helped her take off her coat, wishing he wouldn't have to stop there. Her sweater was soft, fuzzy, and extremely touchable. More importantly, he wanted to explore what lay underneath more than he wanted hot chocolate.

"I should leave," he murmured, torn between going after what he wanted and being noble.

She simply nodded. "That's probably a wise choice."

"I don't want to."

Her voice grew soft. "I don't want you to either."

"What a dilemma. How are we going to resolve it?" he asked as he fingered the few buttons at the neckline of her sweater and slipped them free of their closures.

Cool air caressed her bare skin before his hands did.

"Flip a coin?" she asked.

"Too risky."

Mark's mouth traveled a path down her neck and between her breasts, until she sagged against him.

"I thought you wanted hot chocolate," she whispered, sounding as if her resolve was slipping out of her grasp.

"I do."

"When?" The one word came out on a squeak as he pulled her hips against his.

"For breakfast."

"Should I ask what we'll do until then?"

He raised his head to stare into heavy-lidded eyes dark with passion. "I'm sure we'll dream up something to occupy ourselves."

Dixie smiled. "Like what?"

He undid another button. "Opening packages comes to mind."

She shivered as he caressed her collar-bone. "Packages? What's the occasion?"

"A late Christmas present?"

She leaned against him. "Works for me, but we have a lot of hours to fill."

"True, but some people rip off the wrapping to get inside, while others carefully untie the bows and cut through the tape on each end." He raised the hem of her sweater to bare her midriff before he stroked the skin he'd revealed. "This particular package requires a great deal of care and attention."

"Oh, my," she breathed. "Then this could take a while?"

"Definitely."

She tugged his shirt out of his waistband. "Then I vote for going somewhere a little more private."

Before he could agree, she took his hand and led him into her bedroom. She clicked on the bedside lamp and he turned down the bedspread, noting that although the room hadn't changed much from the night he'd brought in her suitcase, her familiar scent made up for the lack of personal touches.

It didn't matter that the colors were too dark for her—she probably preferred a virginal white eyelet bedspread and curtains to match her sunny personality—because he addressed his attention solely to the woman he took in his arms.

"Where were we?" he asked, before he peeled off her sweater and released the catch on her bra.

"No fair," she murmured. "I have to catch up."

"Be my guest."

His shirt soon joined hers on the floor, but he hardly noticed. He was too busy giving equal attention to her breasts and enjoying the strokes she lavished across his chest.

Her shudder as he teased her nipples with his thumbs sent a fresh surge of blood rushing through him. His control started to slip and the notion of taking his time flew out of the window.

He stood still for a few moments, his muscles rigid as he

tried to harness the raging need that was overtaking him. He'd never felt so utterly consumed by desire and so totally out of control for a woman before. He was old enough and experienced enough to know that this wasn't just a physical response to a beautiful woman. This was something different.

He couldn't adequately describe what it was. How could he express something he hadn't felt before? He only knew that he wanted to hold it with a death-like grip and never let it go.

"How about we speed things up a bit?" he asked before his mouth replaced his hands.

"Please."

The one, breathy word was enough. Slow and easy became fast and furious. Zippers rasped and clothing disappeared until he finally lowered her onto the sheets and continued his gentle assault of her senses until she was moaning beneath him.

"What's…next?"

Her breathiness made him struggle to hold onto the final remnants of his control. And when she moved her hips against his hand, he could no longer deny the temptation of her body.

"This," he said, before he sank inside her and began to move.

"Oh, yes," she murmured, raking her nails down his back. "Oh…*Mark*."

After they'd both reached their climaxes and he held her in his arms, he realized lazily that he'd never felt this contented before in his life. Although the plan was for her to only be in Hope for a short time, he hated the idea of her leaving. Her life was in Chicago, not in Hope, but knowing that didn't stop him from wishing it could be otherwise, at least for a few more months. Now that he'd found someone who'd touched both his body and his soul, he wasn't ready to let her walk out of his life as easily as she'd strolled into it.

For all his rhetoric about how their relationship wouldn't be affected by anyone else because it was between the two of them, he finally admitted that Ned also played a role in the outcome. With luck, though, Ned's part would only be minor

She stirred in his arms. "Talk to me."

He smiled, wondering how she could feel so boneless in his arms and sound so demanding at the same time.

"About what?" he hedged.

"About what's on your mind."

"Who said I had anything on my mind?"

She raised herself on one elbow. "Are you thinking about what happens when Ned comes back?"

Once again, he evaded her question. "Are you?"

"A little."

It was bad enough having Ned's ghost hanging over their heads all day long. He refused to have the specter interfere with his intimate life as well. What happened in the days ahead would happen. In the meantime, he intended to live each moment to the fullest.

"Don't." He pulled her on top of him. "That's an order. This bed, this *room*, is only big enough for the two of us."

She trailed kisses down his neck. "My sentiments exactly."

For the next five days, Dixie lived what she considered the most idyllic life. On Saturday, the weather had warmed considerably, and while the ice melted off the eaves they took a brisk walk through the park. On Saturday night he took her to the bimonthly bingo game where she managed to win a whopping ten dollars.

On Sunday they spent a relaxing day watching old movies on television.

Monday was back to work as usual, although there was nothing usual about passing him in the hallway. She'd been careful not to do anything that might cause Jane or Miranda to speculate on how they'd spent their weekend, but she couldn't stop the heat-filled glances when they were alone.

She should have been thinking about Ned and trying to locate Larissa Grayson, but she was leaning more and more toward letting Ned's chips fall where they may. She was due back at her own job in two weeks and her only concern was how Mark would manage if he didn't have anyone to help him.

As for the idea of falling in love with Mark, these past few days told her that she'd actually done it. She'd passed the point of no return on Friday when they'd spent all night in each other's arms. Just thinking of that special time brought a smile to her lips and sent her heart soaring.

He obviously felt something for her, too, if his attention was any indication. Where their mutual attraction might take them remained to be seen, but she hoped and prayed that her childhood dream of having a family to call her own would come to pass. Maybe it was wishful thinking on her part, but perhaps Ned's situation wouldn't become an insurmountable obstacle.

On Tuesday, she made her morning rounds quite early. To her relief, the cotinine results she'd been waiting for were now on Joey's chart.

She strode into his room and was even more pleased to see both parents with him.

"Good morning," she said cheerily as she wiggled her fingers at Joey who smiled his toothless smile and hid his face in his father's neck.

"He's doing so much better," his mother said.

"He's certainly acting happier," Dixie commented. "Can I listen to your chest, big guy?"

Tom Jamison set Joey on his bed and stood nearby while Dixie pressed her stethoscope against the baby's chest. "All clear," she said.

"Then he can go home?" he asked.

"Yes," Dixie said slowly as she raised the bar on Joey's crib, then she tucked her stethoscope back into the pocket of her lab coat. "But I have some conditions."

He narrowed his eyes suspiciously. "Conditions? What kind of conditions?"

Dixie opened the chart and flipped to the tab marked LAB. "When your son first arrived, I ordered a cotinine test. I don't know if you're familiar with the name or not, but cotinine is a breakdown product of nicotine. Its presence indicates a person's exposure to cigarette smoke.''

''I don't smoke around Joey.''

''The test results show that you do, Mr Jamison.''

''They're wrong,'' he blustered.

She kept her voice even. ''I don't think so. I know you can make your own choices about smoking, but Joey can't.''

''He's not around that much smoke,'' he insisted.

''Your idea of 'not that much' differs from mine,'' she told him.

''A cigarette or two isn't that much.''

''One or two cigarettes don't produce the results I found in Joey's urine.''

''Are you calling me a liar?'' Tom's face turned red and he raised his voice.

In one part of her brain she wondered if Tom was prone to violence. Yet she refused to back down. Joey needed her to fight for him.

''I'm not calling you anything, Tom. I'm simply stating the facts.''

''You're supposed to be treating my son,'' he said belligerently, ''not worrying about the pack or two I go through a day.''

''In order to make Joey well, I *have* to look at everything that contributes to his well-being. He has a history of lung infections and the more often he's exposed to secondhand smoke, the more you place him at risk for suffering what he just went through.''

''He isn't the only kid who got this respiratory virus. I don't know why you're picking on me.''

''I'm not picking on you,'' she told him. ''I'd give the same lecture to every parent who smoked.''

''Yeah, right.''

His attitude was starting to grate on her nerves. ''I agree that Joey isn't the only baby who caught this virus. But he's one of the few whose lungs were already weak and so he had a much harder time fighting his infection.

"The point is," she added calmly, "do you want your son to have healthy lungs or smoker's lungs? Do you want him to catch every respiratory ailment that goes around because his lungs can't stand the extra stress or not?"

"No, we don't," Carrie said, exchanging a glance with her husband. "Do we, Tom?"

"What is with everyone always harassing smokers?" Tom exploded. "Yeah, it's a habit. We all know it. But you doctors aren't perfect. Look at Dr Bentley."

Her ears perked. "What about him?"

"If you want to talk about habits, talk about his. I've seen him around town. If he drinks half of what he carries out of liquor stores, I'm surprised he can walk."

Words failed her. Ned *drank*?

"An occasional drink isn't harmful," she began, hoping she'd heard Tom Jamison incorrectly.

"Occasional?" he scoffed. "My eye. My brother operates a trash service and he says that the good doctor puts out more empties than a bar on Saturday night."

If Tom was right, Ned's situation was worse than she'd ever imagined. As much as she wanted to know more, she felt as if she knew enough.

"We aren't discussing Dr Bentley's habits or lack thereof," she said, determined to regain control of the conversation. "My concern is for Joey and if your habit affects his health, I have to pursue this further."

His eyes narrowed. "What do you mean?"

"I want to see Joey on Friday, in my office, at which time we'll run another cotinine test. We'll continue to do that until I'm assured that he's breathing the best air he possibly can."

"You're rather trusting," Tom jeered. "What's to say I'll bring him to you at all?"

"If he doesn't appear for his appointment, I'll file a child endangerment complaint with Social Services."

His jaw dropped. "You wouldn't."

Dixie looked him straight in the eye. "You can either dea

with me or with the state agency. I'll also give you a tip. I'm far easier to get along with than they are.''

He screwed his face into a frown. For several moments, he didn't answer, until finally, he nodded. ''Joey'll be there.''

Yes, she wanted to shout. Instead, she simply smiled. ''Good. If you're interested in trying nicotine patches, I'll be happy to write a prescription for you.''

Tom looked hard at his son playing in the crib. When Joey pulled off a sock and tried to stuff his foot in his mouth, his expression softened. ''OK. I'll try patches.''

The relief on Carrie's face suggested that she'd been hoping and praying for this moment. Tears glistened in her eyes as she looked at Dixie and mouthed, ''Thank you.''

''I'll write a script for you and the nurse can bring it in when she goes over Joey's home care. I want you to continue with the liquid antibiotics until I see him on Friday. If he runs a fever or develops any problems in the meantime, bring him to my office or the emergency room immediately.''

''I understand.''

''That's it. I'll see you later in the week.''

Dixie strode out of the room, buoyed by her success. Mark would have to monitor both Joey and his father's progress in the weeks and months ahead, but she knew he'd watch them closely.

On the heels of that thought came Tom's accusation about Ned. Was her cousin drinking too much? Or had Jamison simply been trying to switch from a defensive to an offensive strategy?

She wasn't naïve enough to believe that Ned didn't drink at all, but she'd never known or suspected him to drink to excess. Not that her observations counted. She hadn't seen him in nearly a year. A lot could happen in that length of time.

On the other hand, her visits with Ned only lasted for a few hours. He could have easily hidden his addiction from her.

Maybe so, but Mark had been working with him for months

and he'd obviously never suspected that Ned might be an alcoholic. Perhaps Tom Jamison was wrong. Completely wrong.

She hoped so.

Suddenly she had all sorts of questions running through her head. First and foremost was what should she do with this information?

Should she tell Mark what she'd heard? Or should she wait until she had hard evidence and not just the word of an angry man? Why rock the canoe and stir the water for no good reason?

She'd wait, she decided. After she paid a visit to the liquor stores and heard it straight from the employees' mouths, she'd decide what to do next.

Hopefully, she wouldn't have to do anything. Hopefully, this bit of information could die a natural death from lack of substance.

Hopefully, if it was true, Mark would understand.

CHAPTER TEN

"How did it go with the Jamisons?"

Dixie froze at Mark's question. Did he know the bombshell Tom had dropped on her? No, impossible. Mark sounded too casual to be suspicious—he was simply curious.

She almost wished for more patients to see so she could shrug off an answer, but it was five-thirty and the last one had gone home. Miranda had left for an eye appointment and Jane was buried in paperwork. Dixie couldn't expect them to give her an easy out, so she skirted his question. "How did what go?"

"The smoking issue."

"Oh, yeah. That." Her chuckle sounded fake as she clutched an X-ray to her chest when, in truth, she'd been so caught up in her own dilemma that she'd forgotten the one with Joey and his father. "The day's been busy enough that I can hardly remember what I did an hour ago. My visit with the Jamisons went well."

"Tom didn't make a fuss?"

"I wouldn't say that," she admitted. "He wasn't very happy, but after I explained the lab report and how his smoking was affecting his son, he calmed down. He's even agreed to try nicotine patches."

"Whoa. I'm impressed."

"Don't be. It took a little arm-twisting. Actually, a lot of arm-twisting."

His eyes sparkled with merriment. "Oh, yeah? Somehow I can't imagine you being tough."

"Hah! You should see me in my ER. I'll have you know that the drug addicts and gang bangers quake when they see me coming." She raised her nose and pretended affront.

147

"Yeah, right." He sounded as if he was humoring her, which was somewhat irritating. For the most part, she was admittedly, too soft-hearted, but she'd rather he thought of her as tough and competent than a pushover.

"You don't think I can draw a line in the sand and dare someone to cross it?" she asked.

"Maybe. Under the right circumstances."

She squared her shoulders and looked him straight in the eye. "You bet your sweet stethoscope I can. And I did. Tom and his wife will bring Joey in on Friday, come hell or high water."

"What makes you so sure?"

"Because if Joey doesn't show up and if his next cotinine level isn't at zero, they can expect a visit from the county's Social Services worker."

He chuckled. "You *do* play hard ball."

"When I have to."

"Speaking of 'have to,' I have a meeting tonight. The hospital is trying to raise money to build a new helipad with a fund raising Valentine's Day Dance. Believe it or not, I got roped into being on the planning committee."

"Lucky you."

"Want to come along?" he asked hopefully.

"And spend hours listening to everyone's opinion on the way things should be handled?" She shook her head. "Not a chance. Been there, done that."

"If you don't want to attend the meeting, would you come with me to the dance?"

Her pulse skipped a beat. "On Valentine's Day?"

"February 14," he confirmed.

"I thought you already had a date." At his puzzled expression, she added slyly, "With the nurse you called to get Joey admitted to the hospital."

"Oh, her. She's on the planning committee, too. We're all going out for dinner beforehand. It's a couples thing, so you don't want me to be the odd man out, do you?"

Somehow, she doubted if that were possible. "I'd love to," she said, "but—"

"Great. I'm picking up my tickets tonight so I'll snag two instead of one."

"But," she continued on a warning note, "I'm scheduled to report back to work on the tenth."

He straightened to pull her into his embrace. "Maybe you could suffer a relapse. Knees can be tricky."

He obviously knew that when she had his arms around her she couldn't think clearly. The fact that she was willing to fall on any excuse to stay longer only helped her agree to his suggestion. Idly, she wondered how Ned's return would affect her decision, then decided that she didn't care.

"I'll see what I can do," she promised.

"Good." He pressed a hard kiss to her mouth then stepped back. "I'd better go or I'll be late. If this doesn't take all night, can I drop by?"

"Sure. I'll be at home."

"Any special plans?"

Her breath caught in her throat. Did he know that she intended to dust off a few more amateur sleuthing skills? "A few errands," she said instead. "I haven't gone through Ned's papers either, so I'll probably work on those tonight. Why?"

"No reason." He shrugged nonchalantly. "If the meeting gets really boring, I want to imagine what you're doing."

She grinned. "Now probably isn't the time to mention I intend to wear a red lace negligee while I paint my toenails."

He groaned. "If you are, I'm skipping out early."

"No negligees, red or otherwise, are in my closet." The thought of purchasing one on her way home seemed like a good idea, though.

Sighing melodramatically, she added, "I'm just going to lounge in an old pair of jogging pants and a baggy sweatshirt, so you can concentrate strictly on table favors and hors d'oeuvres."

"I'd still rather picture you in a negligee."

She smiled a come-hither smile. "Be my guest."

*   *   *

Dixie trudged into the house well past the dinner hour. She'd stopped at the grocery store for more milk and marshmallows. She'd also dropped into a nearby liquor store and purchased a bottle of wine as her cover for asking questions. The forty-five-year-old owner had been more than happy to help her select a flavorful wine, but the moment she'd mentioned Ned he'd clammed up and stated ''I don't talk about my customers'' in no uncertain terms.

She thought about going to other establishments, but she'd wind up stocking a liquor cabinet in the process. Who was to say that those owners and employees would be any more forthcoming than the first man? The only thing she'd have for her trouble would be sore feet, frozen toes, and more wine than she'd drink in a year.

And what would it matter? Ned could have had any number of legitimate reasons for purchasing the amount of alcohol that Tom Jamison claimed. As Mark had said, Ned had hosted a Christmas party, which could easily explain the liquor store trips and the empty bottles.

She wasn't naïve enough to believe that Ned was a teeto-taler, but if Mark didn't seem to harbor such suspicions, then she shouldn't jump to conclusions either.

As soon as she'd stored her groceries, she visited a few of the nearest neighbors. Unfortunately, they couldn't shed any more light on Ned's whereabouts than the liquor-store owner. In every instance the people mentioned that Ned kept to himself, was friendly when seen, and, although he entertained a lot, no one could complain about him being disruptive.

While part of her was disappointed that she hadn't discovered anything noteworthy, she was also relieved that she had nothing to report. Her relationship with Mark had grown by leaps and bounds, but it remained to be seen where it would go in the long term. Meanwhile, she didn't want anything, not even the mention of her missing cousin, to affect it.

For dinner, she threw together a quick chef salad, then exchanged her trousers and turtleneck sweater for her comfortable jogging pants and sweatshirt. Determined to tackle the papers in Ned's desk, she plugged in her favorite CD and started to work.

It seemed strange to read through someone else's correspondence, but she carried on. If Ned didn't want anyone doing so, he shouldn't have disappeared into thin air.

By the time she'd examined every piece of paper she could find—and wondered if she should pay the bills that were coming due—she'd drawn a clearer picture of her cousin.

She found the usual fees for utilities, rent for the house, and a monthly car payment. He had two credit cards that were maxed, and as far as she could tell most of the expenses listed fell in the entertainment category of hotels, both local and out-of-town restaurants, and clothing. From his bulging closets, she would have guessed the latter even if she hadn't seen his credit-card statement.

All in all, she still had nothing to go on. No names of traveling companions, no photos, no nothing.

Perhaps Mark had been right. Ned had simply decided to splurge on a vacation and with his credit strained to the limit, he'd helped himself to Mark's money.

Her aunt would have to accept Dixie's theory, and if she wasn't satisfied she could hire a professional to look for her son.

Dixie refiled the papers in the places where she'd found them and tackled the stack she'd brought from his desk at the clinic.

Investment information—she wondered why he was interested in the stock market when his bank balance was barely in the black—photocopies of journal articles and Internet printouts of various medical topics formed the bulk of the pile.

One, however, caught her eye. It was a printed report from an Internet source about RU-21, a pill developed by the KGB in the Cold War era to reduce the effects of the next-day hangover.

The question was, did this article hold special significance to Ned or was it simply one of those interesting tidbits one found while surfing the net? She had her own collection of articles, based on their potential for future reference or because they were interesting trivia. Anyone with a suspicious mind who rummaged through her desk drawers might think that she was a potential national threat from the documents she'd amassed on bioterrorism.

She replaced the pages in the same sequence in which she'd found them and sighed. In her opinion, tracking down a disease was far easier than second-guessing a man's thoughts and motives.

Determined to put the whole mess behind her, she took the latest book she'd just bought and crawled into bed even though it was only half past eight. Mark had reluctantly agreed to let her take call this evening and, as busy as the practice had been, she needed to grab her forty winks whenever she could. To do that, however, she had to relax and reading was the best method for her.

Halfway through the second chapter, the phone rang.

"Dr Albright," she answered.

Mark grinned at her crisp, professional tone because he intended to change it. "Hi, Dr Albright. I have this medical emergency."

She chuckled. "What are your symptoms?"

"A sudden craving for something chocolatey and sweet."

"Are you close to a candy machine?"

"Nope. No candy machine. I'm thirsty, too."

"Sounds serious. It might even be life-threatening."

"I thought so. What's your prescription, Doctor?"

"Stop at the convenience store and buy a cappuccino."

"No hot chocolate at Chez Albright?"

"The kitchen's closed, I'm afraid. I'm already in bed. Waiting for you, I might add."

Picturing her in a slinky nightgown with the sheets tangled around her and the comforter in a heap, he groaned. "I wish you hadn't told me that."

"Want to guess what I'm wearing?"

"You found a red negligee?" If she said that she'd bough

one, he'd claim a real medical emergency and leave during the short break they'd taken.

"No such luck. I'm tucked up nice and neat in my sweat-shirt and jogging pants, so cool your jets, Captain."

"If you insist."

"How's your meeting?"

"We're taking a break right now. We had to sample all the possible menu items before we could decide what we wanted."

"You've been gorging yourself on hors d'oeuvres?"

"It's a tough job, but somebody has to do it."

Her laugh made him smile. "I'll bet. How much longer will you be?"

"Another hour or so. Have you had any calls?"

"Just yours," she assured him.

"If you need anything, you know how to reach me."

"Your number is in my cellphone."

He hadn't realized she'd done so, but it smacked of a per-manence that he liked. "They're getting ready to start again so I have to go."

"Are you discussing the party favors next?"

"We've already taken care of those. Now we have to find a different band. The group we'd booked has canceled, which means we'll be calling until we find one. It could take hours."

"Then I shouldn't wait for you?"

"No."

"Darn." Her disappointment reverberated in that single word, but it didn't come close to matching his.

"I'll see you tomorrow," he promised. "Sweet dreams."

Mark closed his phone with a snap and turned to find an-other medical colleague, Justin St James, wearing a smirk on his handsome face.

"Checking in with the little woman?" Justin teased.

"Get a life," Mark told his friend without rancor. He, Galen, Jared, and Justin had formed a band of brothers when they'd first moved to Hope because they'd been the only four unmarried physicians in town. Their bond had solidified when

they'd survived last summer's plane crash. While Jared and
Galen had now joined the ranks of the married, he and Justin
were still unattached.

"I hear your locum is quite a dish," Justin remarked.

"Don't bother adding her to your flavor of the month
club," Mark informed him. "She's already occupied."

"So I hear." Justin's eyes twinkled. Although he hadn't
found the woman he wanted to settle down with, he didn't
poach on another man's territory, so Mark felt reasonably safe
that he wouldn't horn in on Dixie.

"I must say, old man," Justin continued. "I think I'm be-
ginning to rub off on you. I've never known you to go after
a locum, considering how temporary they are."

"She isn't a locum." At Justin's raised eyebrow, he continued, "She is, but she isn't. She's Ned Bentley's cousin."

Justin stared at him in horror. "Oh, man. Have I taught you
nothing? You're smack dab in the middle of one ugly situation. Next thing you know, Bentley'll be leading you around
by the nose and she'll have you by the—"

"It isn't like that. It won't *be* like that. She's leaving right
after the Valentine's Day dance."

Justin shrugged. "If you say so." He clapped a hand on
Mark's shoulder. "Be careful, bud. You've been burned before."

As if Mark needed a reminder, or a warning. "She might
be the one, though," he said, trying the idea on for size and
realizing that it didn't fit too badly.

"She might. Just remember that falling for your partner's
cousin could either make your life heaven or hell. If it works
for you, great, but this situation is far too complicated for my
blood."

"She said the same thing."

"She did?" Justin appeared surprised. "Then she's a smart
woman. Whatever you do, don't rush into anything."

"I won't." Mark took his seat at the conference table and
thought about the turn his life had taken. No matter how well
his life meshed with Dixie's, no matter how often he advised

her to take each day at a time, and no matter what Ned had done, they couldn't discuss or even hint at a future until the louse returned.

The fact was, he wanted her to stay in Hope indefinitely, preferably for ever. Justin's admonitions to be careful and not to rush into anything had come too late.

He had fallen in love with Dixie.

By the end of her second week in Hope, Dixie felt as if her life in Chicago belonged to someone else. Once in a while she missed the hustle and bustle of the ER, but because of her experience she'd willingly accepted the assignment of ER back-up call. Galen and his wife, Nicole, served as ER backup during the day, but evenings and nights were covered by a rotating call schedule and she'd willingly offered her services. Twice now she'd gone in to help Jared and the rotating docs, once after her office hours had ended at five and once at midnight on a Saturday night. Both cases had been MVAs— motor vehicle accidents—involving four or more people, but they'd all lived to see another day.

Her appointment with the Jamisons had gone like clock-work. She'd collected a urine sample from Joey for another cotinine level and Tom grudgingly admitted that his patches seemed to be helping, for the most part.

After encouraging him not to give up on them, she sent the young family on their way. While it was too soon to pat herself on the back for a complete victory, she felt they were headed in the right direction.

On her way to her next patient, Miranda stopped her in the hallway. "Phone call, Doctor."

"Can you take a message?"

"The woman was extremely insistent. I believe she said she was your aunt."

Dixie snapped her fingers. "Darn. I forgot to call her yes-erday. I'll take it in my office."

"Line three."

"Thanks."

A minute later Dixie sank onto her chair, took a bracing breath, then punched the blinking light. "Aunt Cora? How are you?"

"Oh, Dixie," her aunt gushed. "I have the most wonderful news."

At least she wasn't complaining because Dixie hadn't produced any leads on her son. "What is it?"

"Why, Ned phoned me about thirty minutes ago."

Her aunt couldn't have told her anything more surprising. "He did? Where is he? What has he been doing? When is he coming back?"

"Hold on, dear. I have to tell this in my own way or I'll forget everything he said."

Dixie pressed her lips together and counted to ten. "OK. What did he say?"

"He's at a treatment center in Seattle."

"Treatment? What sort of treatment?"

"Mind you, he doesn't really have a problem. Oh, he drinks, but he's not an alcoholic. I don't care what those people say, he's my son and I'd know if he was."

Her aunt had confirmed what Dixie hadn't wanted to believe, but she didn't say a word. She couldn't.

"He wouldn't be there now," she continued, "but his tramp of a girlfriend threatened to turn him in to the state Board of Healing Arts if he didn't go for an evaluation. Once he was there, those people simply *refused* to let him leave. They shouldn't be able to do that, should they?"

Dixie was well aware of how those programs worked. One of her fellow ER physicians had had a similar problem with prescription drugs. He'd gone for an evaluation and once there he'd had to complete the treatment program if he wanted to continue practicing medicine. The potential of losing one's livelihood created a powerful incentive.

"They do," she said dryly. "It's for our patients' protection."

"Still, that woman should be flogged," her aunt insisted. "How dare she put Ned through this? Put *us* through this?"

Sensing her aunt's diatribe would continue if she allowed it to, Dixie steered the conversation onto a slightly different course. "When will they release him?"

"If I understood Ned correctly, about ten days."

A little over a week. Ten days until she had no reason to remain in Hope. She should have been happy to return to Chicago, but she wasn't.

"Which brings me to my reason for calling you," her aunt said. "Ned wants you to make sure he has a job when he returns. Talk to his boss, Martin Campbell."

"Mark Cameron," Dixie corrected. "I've already done all I can, but it's out of my hands."

"Nonsense. All you have to do is say that Ned had to get away and he'll return around the first of the month."

"Had to get away?" Dixie echoed. "That excuse won't cut it. Mark has lived through hell trying to keep up with his practice by himself. He deserves to know the truth."

"But we can't tell him the truth. He might not want Ned to work there if he knows about Ned's little problem."

"Ned's problem isn't little. Mark needs to know."

"Nonsense. What difference does it make if Ned performs his job? He's quite capable, you know."

"You don't understand. If Ned should start drinking and make a mistake, the liability will be horrendous."

Her aunt's voice grew hard. "Ned was adamant. His boss is not to know about his alcohol problem. If this Cameron person finds out, we'll know exactly who told him."

"I can't lie. I *won't* lie. This isn't right and I won't let Ned do this to Mark—Dr Cameron."

"Is this the thanks we get for bringing you into our home? That you won't help Ned in his hour of need?"

In that instant Dixie replayed her efforts on Ned's behalf over the years. What she'd done under the guise of helping or looking after her relatives had been the crutch that Mark had already pointed out. However, no matter how anyone described it, her actions could have been textbook examples of enabling behavior. By rushing in to rescue Ned from himself, she'd supported his destructive habits.

It was time for the cycle to stop.

"Ned got himself into this and he has to get himself out of it. He's the only one who can smooth things over. Considering he stole a lot of money from Mark, he has to make restitution."

"Nonsense." Dixie cringed at her aunt's favorite word. "I know about the missing money, but if you pay off the debt, what can Cameron do? He'll have his money, which is all he's interested in, I'm sure."

"I'm not a bank."

"No, but you have money in your trust fund," her aunt said slyly. "More than enough to cover the amount Ned borrowed. He'll work out a schedule with you to repay every dime."

Her aunt's reassurances did little to calm Dixie's reservations about Ned's ability or his interest in reimbursing her. He'd borrowed far lower amounts from her over the years and she had yet to see a single cent.

"No, Aunt Cora. I won't do that. Ned has to pay his own debts. I won't be the middle man."

"Well." Her aunt sniffed. "I hadn't realized you'd become so ungrateful. After everything we've done for you, how can you turn your back on your cousin?"

"I'm not ungrateful. Ned is old enough to take responsibility for his own actions. Maybe if I hadn't stepped in so often, he wouldn't be in this predicament."

"Then you're not going to help him now." She stated it as a fact.

"I *am* helping him," Dixie insisted. "Just not in the way you think I should. Ned needs to repay Mark on his own, but first he has to call and explain where he is and why."

"Ned won't agree. He doesn't want anyone to know. Why, if word got out about his drinking, his reputation would suffer Who would want him in their practice or treating their patients?"

"Who will want him if he kills a patient because he couldn't function at the time?" Dixie countered. "It's too late for secrets. Ned, not you or me, has to talk to Mark."

"Why must we air our dirty laundry to strangers?" her aunt groused. "What purpose will it serve?"

"Without honesty, what's left?" Mark's words echoed in her mind. "I'll give Ned one week to call Mark."

"A week?"

"Seven days," she affirmed. "Ned obviously has access to a phone or he couldn't have contacted you. And if he doesn't, he needs to write a long letter. Either way, he has to be open and truthful."

"And what if Ned chooses not to say anything about his alcohol problem?"

She'd never dreamed her family would force her into an ultimatum. "Then I'll tell Mark everything. If I do, I can guarantee that Ned won't have a job."

A pregnant pause filled the air waves.

"Fine," her aunt snapped. "I'll tell Ned he has one week. However, if this situation backfires, I'm holding you personally responsible. You will no longer be considered a member of this family."

Dixie tried not to reflect on the years she'd tried to gain their acceptance. What happened happened. She'd survived the loss of her family before, she'd survive the loss of this one, too.

"One week," Dixie repeated. "I'll be waiting."

She broke the connection, then cradled her face in her hands. This entire situation was worse than she'd expected, worse than she'd ever imagined. She'd been so naïve to think Ned's disappearance had been a simple case of being involved in a car accident and laid up in a hospital, unable to contact anyone.

How dared Ned expect to hide his problem from his boss? And how *dared* both he and his mother expect her to fix the royal mess Ned had made? This wasn't a case of a missed car or rent payment. This was serious business. As far as she was concerned, whatever Mark chose to do was fine with her.

In the meantime, she had her own problems to sort out.

She jumped to her feet and caught Mark as he was between patients. "May I have a word with you?" she asked, trying to sound calm and matter-of-fact when she was the opposite.

"I have a patient waiting," he began.

"So do I. This won't take long."

Clearly puzzled by her request, he opened the nearest door and motioned her inside. "Is this OK?"

"It's fine." Dixie drew a deep breath. "I made a terrible mistake."

He didn't seem shocked. Instead, he leaned against the counter. "Whatever it is, it probably isn't as terrible as you think, but I'm listening."

She drew a shaky breath. "When I first learned about the money Ned took, I wanted to repay you. So I contacted my lawyer and arranged a transfer out of my trust fund to your bank account."

"I see."

"I didn't do it for Ned. Well, maybe a little part of me wanted to right the wrong, but I felt more badly for you. It bothered me when you took out the loan that Ned should have taken, and you were paying the price. Then, when the windows were broken, I thought I'd done the right thing to help you. It seemed silly to make you struggle when I had the means available to make your life a little easier."

"Then you had second thoughts," he guessed.

"Yes, but not because I stopped wanting to help you. The night of the vandalism, I saw how you handled the situation with Robbie and I understood what you'd been saying all along. Ned has to suffer his own consequences. Whatever they might be."

"I appreciate your honesty," he said gently. "This means more than you know."

She wanted to weep. She didn't want him to be impressed by what she'd done, because it only made her feel worse.

"I would have said something sooner, but I forgot," she said, clearing the lump out of her throat. "I...er, I remembered today, and decided to tell you before Jane opened your next bank statement and you wondered where the money had come from. As I said, I still would like to help you. If you'd like to consider it as a loan that's fine, or if you want to return it I don't care."

"What about Ned?"

She managed a smile. "As you've told me before, this is between you two. I'm staying out of it."

"Good girl. You know I'll return the full amount to you."

She nodded. "I thought as much."

He straightened. "I'll ask Jane to contact the bank and write you a check."

"Whatever. Thanks for...understanding."

Dixie fled. At least she'd dealt with her mistake. Only time would tell if Ned would deal with his.

CHAPTER ELEVEN

MARK watched Dixie leave as if rabid dogs nipped at her heels. She'd clearly been uncomfortable about coming to him and admitting to taking matters in her own hands but, as he'd told her, he appreciated her honesty. She could have simply let him find the money on his own or, worse yet, let him think that Ned had paid his debt.

Whatever her reason, he'd fully expected her to cover Ned's theft if it had been in her power. She'd cleaned up Ned's messes before, so he wasn't surprised that she'd done it again.

What *did* surprise him, though, and what was far more important to him, was what truly lay at the heart of her admission.

She trusted him.

If he'd ever clung to the doubt that Dixie was simply trying to manipulate him, her simple actions said otherwise.

The love he'd been trying to hold at bay refused to be denied. His hesitation to get involved, to risk being in a position where someone he cared for could exploit his feelings for her own agenda, faded. He wanted Dixie to be a part of his life, today and for ever. Yes, there were still complications—his day of reckoning with Ned—but right now Mark didn't consider any problem insurmountable.

He found Jane. "Call the bank and check our account balance."

She frowned. "I can give it to you right now. It's in my ledger."

"No," he said. "Call the bank. Dixie transferred money into our account."

Jane turned bug-eyed. "She did?"

"Yeah. I want you to reimburse her for the same amount."

"You're not keeping it?"

He shook his head. "Not one cent."

Jane wrinkled her brow and looked at him as if he'd lost his mind. Maybe he had. "You're sure."

"Absolutely."

"OK, but I don't understand."

"It's not her debt and she knows it."

"But…you're so…*calm* about this."

"Would you rather I bellowed at the top of my lungs about her audacity? Or yelled and screamed because I was giving the money back?"

"No-o-o."

He smiled. "Then just write the damn check so I can give it to her."

Jane's gaze became speculative. "You like her, don't you?"

"I like all of my staff."

She shot him a get-serious look. "I meant, you *really* like her."

No, he didn't. He loved her. However, Dixie would be the first one to hear that. Not Jane.

"You aren't dialing," he reminded her with a wink.

Jane giggled, as if she knew that he wasn't going to admit anything to anyone at the moment, then picked up the receiver. "One phone call coming right up."

Saturday rolled into Sunday and then Monday. The weather had warmed to above freezing and the snow and ice were slowly turning to slush as the pristine white ground turned to a muddy, sloppy gray.

Dixie, however, didn't notice. She was determined to live to the fullest the days until Ned returned. Who knew what would happen when the two men confronted each other? If they did at all.

She'd warned Ned, through her aunt, to be honest with Mark. Ned wasn't the first physician to suffer from an addiction problem, neither would he be the last, but he simply had to admit his weakness to his boss. As she'd already told Aunt Cora, if Ned didn't, then Dixie would. Ned would be in for a big surprise if he thought he could bluff his way out of this and still receive Mark's mercy.

Although Dixie had outlined what she would do, she knew that following through would be the hardest thing she'd ever done. Protecting Ned was so ingrained in her that she couldn't bear to watch him throw his life away.

At times she caught herself wanting to phone her aunt and retract her ultimatum, but she'd look at Mark and realize that if she did she'd disappoint herself. She was a physician, with a duty to treat people's illnesses, and if she didn't stand firm, she was allowing Ned to remain active in his disease of chemical dependency.

If she caved in to her aunt's pressure, Mark's disappointment would be twice as difficult for her to handle. On the other hand, was Mark's approval worth the guaranteed loss of her family if she interfered?

The demon of doubt whispered in her ear. *Why get involved one way or another? This is between Mark and your cousin.*

It was, and she would stay out of this as long as possible. But she couldn't let her cousin sweep this under the rug. If anything happened to a patient as a result of his dependency, she would never forgive herself.

The only thing she could do was hope Ned would see the light. Hope that his counselors would convince him that her plan was the right way to go. Hope that she wouldn't have to say a single word to Mark.

Meanwhile, she would try not to think about upholding her end of her threat and what it would do to her relationship with her family. That, however, was easier said than done.

On Thursday, Mark stopped her in the hallway. "Jared and Annie invited us over to their place for drinks before the Valentine's Day dinner and dance. Is that OK with you?"

She'd completely forgotten about the Valentine's Day festivities. "Yeah, sure. Sounds like fun."

He studied her through slightly narrowed eyes. "Is something wrong?"

Dixie pasted on a bright smile. "What makes you say that?"

"I don't know. You've seemed preoccupied the past few days."

Her laugh sounded forced. "Preoccupied?"

"Yeah. I know you're concerned about not finding this Larissa Grayson—"

"No," she denied. "Not really. Like you said. Hope is a small town. She'll turn up eventually."

"If you're worried about Ned—"

"I'm not," she answered quickly. "You haven't heard from him, have you?"

From his expression, she knew she'd surprised him with her question. "No. Did you think I would?"

She shrugged. "I'd hoped. He's been gone nearly, what, four weeks?"

"Four plus."

"I truly expected him to contact you."

"Then you're the only one," he said.

Which meant that her seven-day ultimatum would end tomorrow at noon. If she gave Ned a grace period, she could stretch it until five p.m., but either way he had approximately twenty-four hours to meet her conditions. Although her stomach knotted at the prospect of going to Mark, she would.

At the same time, she hoped she wouldn't have to explain why she'd held this information to herself for a week.

Neither Ned nor her aunt probably expected her to show any backbone because it was so completely out of character. They both knew how important the idea of family was to her.

This time, however, she'd stand firm. She might have done everything they'd asked of her out of respect for Aunt Cora being her mother's sister, but if she didn't do the right thing now, she'd lose her self-respect.

And that was more important because she had to live with herself.

Suddenly aware of Mark's curious scrutiny, she injected a light-hearted note into her voice. "If I seem a little distracted, it's because I'm thinking about going back to Chicago in a couple of weeks."

He frowned. "You're staying for the fourteenth, aren't you?"

"Oh, yes. I've worked that out." Her boss had been concerned about her knee, but she'd simply assured him that she was healing nicely. She wanted a few more days of vacation and because she had plenty of accrued leave she had decided to cash in a few more days now, rather than later.

His gaze grew intent. "You don't have to go back. You could stay here."

She'd love that more than anything, but making plans right now was foolhardy at best.

"I'm not a family practice physician," she pointed out.

"You've been covering in the ER."

"Only as back-up. I need to work more than one night a week." She smiled a grateful smile that he'd even suggested it. "I'm not independently wealthy, you know."

"Fairview is only forty miles away. They have a hospital and an ER."

The town he'd mentioned was half the size of Hope. She knew, because several of their patients lived in Fairview and commuted to Hope for their jobs.

"It's something to consider," she said noncommittally.

"Something else to consider is for us to pool our resources."

Pool their resources? "Meaning what?" she asked, not wanting to misunderstand. "Moving in together?"

"Yeah."

She would have preferred something more permanent, but his failed engagement had obviously made him a little gun-shy. The fact that he'd asked this of her when they'd only known each other such a short time was more than she'd allowed herself to dream.

"I'll have to check into my job prospects before I can answer,'' she said honestly. ''Speaking of prospects, what time is your interview with Dr Bennington this afternoon?''

''Four o'clock.''

''His résumé looks promising.''

''I think so, too. It helps that both he and his wife want to raise their three kids in a relatively small community.''

''I hope he'll be a good match.''

''That makes two of us.''

At three forty-five, Mark introduced Dixie to his newest applicant. Dixie was immediately impressed by the doctor's calm manner and easy smile. His reply to Mark's announcement about their overworked practice only sealed her opinion.

''Don't let this gray hair fool you,'' John said in obvious reference to the silver at his temples. ''Having three kids in four years is to blame. If I can run after them, I can handle whatever workload we have here.''

While the two men closeted themselves in Mark's office, Dixie continued with business as usual. By the time she'd sent the last patient home at five-thirty, the men had come out wearing pleased smiles on their faces.

''I'm taking John and his wife to dinner,'' Mark told her while John went to another room to use his cellphone. ''Can you join us?''

''I'm not sure if I should. I don't want John to think that he needs to impress me, too, in order to get the job.''

''He won't. I want you there because I value your opinion.''

''If I'm wrong, you're the one who has to live with him,'' she warned.

''True, but what do you think of him so far?''

''No fair,'' she protested. ''I may have read his curriculum vitae, but I barely said hello.''

''Would it help if I mentioned that I offered him the job?''

''You did?''

He grinned. ''Yeah. He's going to talk it over with his wife and let me know in the next couple of days. Tonight is just a pleasant dinner between colleagues.''

"Then I accept."

By the time they'd ended the meal and the Benningtons had returned to their hotel for the night, Dixie knew that Mark had chosen well in John Bennington.

While she told herself that hiring John didn't affect Ned's position, she still wondered what the future held. She'd been tempted to ask why Mark didn't wait for Ned's return so that he could be involved in the decision, but she stopped herself. Mark believed he faced weeks of working alone. Under those circumstances, he couldn't let a qualified physician slip through his fingers, neither did she want him to.

Mark had promised to listen to Ned's story and she trusted that he would. What Ned's story would be posed her next question because, depending on the answer, her cousin could draw her into the middle of a very nasty situation.

Shortly after they both arrived at the practice on Friday morning, Miranda handed Mark a message.

"Dr Tremaine called from the ER. One of our patients is there with a suspected miscarriage. He wanted to let you know."

Mark glanced at the clock. He had forty-five minutes before his first appointment. "Did he say who it was?"

"He hung up before I could ask. I got the impression he didn't have time to chat."

"All right. I'll be back as soon as I can."

The ER was as busy as Saturday at midnight. "An early morning MVA," a harried nurse explained. "Dr Tremaine has been busy with the two involved. He hopes you don't mind looking after your patient."

Mark didn't. This was how small community emergency departments worked. "Where's the chart?"

"Here." The nurse handed it to him. "Room three."

He glanced at name and his pulse raced. Larissa Grayson!

"Larissa," he said as he entered her cubicle. "I'm Doctor…" He stopped short at seeing her familiar face lying against the white sheets. "June?"

This was even better. He knew that Ned had dated this woman because he'd met her.

"Hi, Mark," she said weakly.

"I must have the wrong room. I'm looking for Larissa Grayson."

"I know. That's me." She smiled weakly. "I use my middle name with my friends."

He smiled. "No problem. Is it all right if I call you June?"

"Please."

"The nurse says you think you're miscarrying?"

Suddenly June's face crinkled and she burst into tears. "Yes. It's all my fault. I've been so upset and now I'm bleeding…"

"Let's back up a minute. Tell me exactly how much?"

"I can't tell for sure. It alternates between moderate and light. I'm losing the baby, aren't I?"

He patted her arm. "Don't panic yet. We'll run a sonogram and blood tests. After we have those results, we'll have a better idea of what's going on."

Now wasn't the time to quiz her about Ned—the baby demanded her concern and his. Other questions could come later.

After the lab technician drew June's blood sample and the radiology tech ran the sonogram, Mark sat beside her bed. "The sono films still show your baby is right where he or she should be. As soon as I get the beta-HCG report from the lab, which is a hormone that is produced by the developing fetus, I'll either admit you or send you home on bed rest."

She nodded.

"You mentioned earlier that you'd been upset. Are you—?"

"Oh, Mark," she moaned before her face crumpled. "I've made such a mess of things."

"What things?"

"The baby is Ned's."

He didn't know what to say. "Ned's?" he echoed.

"Yes. He wasn't very happy when I told him, especially

when I said that our baby deserved a father who didn't crawl into a bottle every night."

"Crawl into a bottle?" he asked, aware that the phrase usually referred to someone who drank heavily.

Her story poured out and Mark could only listen.

"At night, he would drink constantly. I never saw him drunk, but I was worried about him. I told him that he was an alcoholic, but he denied it. How could he *believe* that he didn't have a problem when he'd disappear for several days to hole up in a hotel and drink? Normal people don't do that."

That explained Ned's three-day vacations. But if Ned drank heavily, how could he himself not have noticed? Had he missed some sign, or had the indications stared him in the face and he'd subconsciously refused to believe?

"I finally convinced him to prove he wasn't an alcoholic by going to a drug treatment facility in Seattle that caters to physicians. He was only supposed to stay there for a few days for an evaluation, but once he was there they wouldn't let him leave. They said if he left, they'd take away his license."

She wiped her tear-streaked cheeks. "I just wanted him to straighten himself out. Not lose everything he's worked for."

"Did he stay?"

She shook her head. "Yes, but he was furious with me. He hasn't talked to me since he called to say he had to complete the program."

"Those facilities aren't free," he said, already guessing where Ned had found the money.

"I know," she said miserably, "which only makes it worse because he can't afford it."

"He couldn't afford *not* to go there," Mark said kindly.

"I wanted to tell you, but I was afraid you'd be angry for my part in all this. With Ned gone, I know you've been working yourself to death. And then when I found out that Ned's cousin, Dr Albright, was here, I was even more scared to tell anyone."

"Did you look after Ned's house?" he asked.

"Yeah, until I learned that Dr Albright had moved in."

June had cleared up the entire mystery. "You did the right thing," Mark told her. "If Ned has a problem, treatment is the best thing for him and for his patients. Remember that, no matter what he says or does. If you need help with anything, let me know."

She sniffled. "Thanks, Mark."

He rose. "Do you know when they'll release him?"

"Any day. Monday at the latest."

Which meant that he only had a day or two alone with Dixie. A day or two when Ned wouldn't complicate their relationship.

No, that wasn't right. Mark simply wouldn't *allow* Ned to complicate his relationship with Dixie. As for his professional association with Dixie's cousin, that remained to be seen. He'd promised Dixie that he'd listen to Ned's side of the story, and he would.

In the meantime, he couldn't wait to tell Dixie where her cousin had been all this time. The lost had been found.

The cubicle door opened and a nurse handed over a report. "This just came in," she said before she slipped away as quietly as she'd appeared.

He read the figures. "Good news," he said with a smile. "The numbers are where they should be for the gestational date indicated on the sonogram."

June sighed with relief.

"To be on the safe side, I want to repeat this test on Monday. From now until then I want you to go home and stay off your feet."

"And the bleeding?"

"I suspect that you've experienced some spontaneous bleeding due to the changes your body is undergoing. If it doesn't get any worse, we're OK. If it does, come back in."

"I will."

Mark rehearsed his announcement all the way back to his practice's offices. Dixie would be so relieved to know that her wayward cousin hadn't been lying in an intensive care unit in some godforsaken place. On the other hand, he couldn't deny that he felt somewhat responsible for not noticing Ned's problem.

On the heels of that thought, he wondered if Ned's drinking had ever affected his judgment. Mark hadn't heard of any complaints, but word didn't always get around. Nor had he made a practice of looking over Ned's shoulder.

The repercussions of Ned's habit hit him like a sledgehammer. Yet what was done was done. His next order of business was to protect his practice and his patients.

"Where's Dixie?" he asked Jane as soon as he arrived.

"Last time I saw her, she was in the med room."

Mark strode in that direction like a man with a mission. In his experience, the best way to handle bad news was to simply spell it out.

"Mark!" Dixie's face lit up as soon as she saw him. "You're back. How's the patient?"

"Larissa Grayson is doing fine. She's not losing the baby."

Shock replaced her smile. "Larissa? Oh my goodness. Did you get a chance to—"

"She's pregnant with Ned's baby," he said wearily. "I knew her and didn't realize it. When I met her last November, Ned introduced her as June."

"That's one question answered."

"So is the one of where Ned's been for the past month," he said flatly.

Her expression grew wary. "Oh?"

"He's in a drug treatment facility. Apparently June knew he drank too much and talked him into going for an evaluation. Once he was there, they wouldn't let him leave."

Mark didn't know what sort of reaction to expect, but he certainly hadn't anticipated her lack of surprise or relief.

"June said he'll be coming home some time this weekend."

Again, her lack of response bothered him, especially the way she avoided his gaze and the way her cheeks flushed with embarrassment or…guilt? If he didn't know better, he'd suspect…

Playing his growing hunch, he added, "But you probably knew that already, didn't you?"

Unable to lie to him, Dixie could only nod. "Yes."

He paused. "For how long?"

"A week."

"A week?" His shocked puzzlement gave way to anger. "When were you going to tell me, or didn't you think it *important* enough to tell me?" he snarled.

"My aunt told me last Friday when she telephoned. She didn't want me to say anything—"

"A suggestion you obviously obeyed," he interrupted.

"She didn't want me to say a word," she went on, "but I informed her that Ned simply had to tell you everything. He didn't want to, but I insisted."

He crossed his arms. "Yeah, well, he plainly doesn't care what you *insist* on."

"I gave him until noon today to call you, at which time I would tell you myself."

"So you say."

"It's true," she persisted. "According to my aunt, he didn't plan to discuss his alcohol problems with you at all. I was just giving him time to work up the courage."

"Time to think of a way to cover for him more likely."

"No!" She was aghast. "That wasn't my intention. I knew you'd be fair if you heard his side of the story. I only wanted him to be the one to give it to you. You didn't want me to fight his battles, remember?"

"You should have told me a week ago. I still would have listened to him. Or didn't you trust me?"

"Of course I did," she said hotly, furious that Mark was so quick to believe the worst. "You said yourself that I shouldn't get involved. What happened between you two was your concern, not mine. I was trying to follow your own instructions by staying out of the middle."

"You've been in the middle since you arrived, though, haven't you? Coming here, determined to hold his job for him."

"At first, yes. Was it so terribly wrong to ask you to give him a second chance?"

He didn't answer for a long moment, but when he spoke his voice was cold. "I only have one question. Was everything between us a lie? Were you only acting as Ned's insurance policy? Playing me like a fiddle?"

"No. Never," she said vehemently. Then, because he didn't seem convinced, she added, "Please, Mark. You have to believe me. Our relationship happened in spite of Ned, not because of him."

"Sorry, but I don't quite believe you. Know this. Trust is a two-way street and right now I don't trust you any more than I trust Ned."

A stabbing wouldn't have hurt nearly as badly as his words did.

"I'm sorry you feel that way," she said stiffly. "But perhaps my trust in you was misguided as well. I should have known you'd operate under a double standard."

"I do not—" he protested.

She cut him off. "If you don't mind, I'd like to finish my work for the day so I can leave. For good."

"Fine."

Dixie blinked away the tears brimming in her eyes. She wouldn't let him see that he'd crushed her spirits to a fine powder. She had her pride, too, and she drew the remnant of it around her like a tattered cloak. Before she could stride past Mark, a familiar voice stopped her in her tracks.

"Well, now, this looks like a happy gathering."

She gazed at the man standing in the doorway, hardly able to believe her eyes. "Ned?"

"In the flesh." He waltzed in, impeccably dressed, his light brown hair neatly trimmed and combed. Standing next to Mark, however, she realized that he didn't measure up to the man she loved in either stature or character.

"The prodigal has returned," Mark commented dryly.

"Absolutely." Ned addressed Dixie. "Thanks for covering for me, Dix. I'll take over now."

"Covering?" she sputtered. Why, he made it sound as if this had all been planned.

"Sure. I appreciate you filling in. Now you can go back to Chicago and your stabbings and shootings. I'm sure life in Hope was pretty dull for you."

"It wasn't dull," she ground out. "As for filling in—"

Mark interrupted, his voice surprisingly even. "Where've you been all this time, Ned?"

Ned glanced at Dixie. "Why, didn't you tell him? I went to Mexico. This little mission down there was desperate for medical expertise, so I volunteered at the last minute."

"Mexico. Really?" Mark sounded interested, almost impressed.

Dixie's mouth dropped. How could Ned have thought up such a crazy story? He had plainly dismissed her ultimatum, and from the single glare he shot at her before he turned on his charm he clearly expected her to support his charade.

Well, she wouldn't.

"Ned, be honest. We all know—"

"I never thought you were interested in helping Third World villages," Mark said in a tone that suggested he was only toying with his colleague. "I'm sure they'll be happy to hire you for full-time duty."

"Oh, but I couldn't."

Mark shrugged. "If you can't, you can't. Either way, you're not working here."

The surprise on Ned's face was priceless, and if Dixie hadn't felt so whipped by her encounter with Mark, she might have laughed. "I'm not?"

"No. Although I suspect that serving a village's medical needs is far better than being in prison."

"What?" From the way Ned glanced at Mark, then at Dixie and back again, he could have been watching a tennis match.

"We know about your alcohol problem," Mark said. "And I know about the money."

"I'll pay you back," he said sulkily.

"If you want to stay out of jail, you'll take care of your debt before you leave."

"You can't fire me. That's discrimination."

"I'm not terminating you because of your addiction. We could have worked around that. As for the money, we could have worked something out for that, too, but we're not. And do you know why?" He didn't wait for Ned to answer. "Because you weren't honest, and as a result I can't trust you. A lie, whether intentional or by omission, is still a lie."

Dixie winced at Mark's accusation. Why couldn't he understand her position? She'd only been trying to do the right thing for Ned by staying out of the middle. Instead, she'd ended there anyway.

"You have until noon to clear out your things." Mark's gaze went from Ned to Dixie, and she knew that she was included in his order. "That gives you a couple of hours. I suggest you use them wisely."

CHAPTER TWELVE

MARK stormed into his office, furious by what he saw as Dixie's perfidy. She'd claimed to trust him to do the right thing, and yet, when the chips had been down, she'd still insisted on protecting Ned.

To think he'd asked her to move in with him. To think that she was different than Andrea. To think that they could have had a future. He'd been such a fool to fall for another pretty face and a winsome smile.

A brisk knock at the door brought him out of his mental tirade. "Come," he yelled.

Miranda marched in. "What's all the ruckus? Everyone in a two-block area can hear you."

"I fired Ned and Dixie is leaving. End of story."

"That might be the end, but there's a lot more to it than that. Jane and I heard every word."

"Then if you know, why ask?"

"Because you need to talk about it—get whatever is eating you out of your system."

"Dixie lied to me. She knew where Ned was and didn't tell me."

"So?" she said bluntly. "What purpose would it have served? Wouldn't you have accused her of bailing him out? Of protecting him so that he wouldn't have to acknowledge his own actions?"

He opened his mouth to disagree, then closed it with a snap. "I don't know."

"Well, I do. That's exactly what you would have done. She was placed in a no-win situation. If the truth be known, I'll bet her aunt put a ton of pressure on her."

From Dixie's description of her family, Mark didn't doubt

it. However, her aunt's threats still didn't excuse her actions, he thought irritably.

"And are you sure that she wouldn't have told you?" Miranda asked. "She'd set her time limit for Dr Bentley to contact you at noon. One thing about Dixie—she stands by her word."

He didn't answer. In the short time he'd known her, Dixie had never done anything to suggest otherwise.

"In case your watch is broken, she still had a few hours to go," she added. "If you ask me—"

"I'm not," he said dryly.

"Too bad, because you'll hear my opinion anyway. Dixie crawled under your skin and into your heart, but you've been waiting for her to betray you like Andrea did."

"I have not."

"Maybe not consciously, but deep down I think part of you expected something like this. Now that it has happened, or you *think* it has, you're using this minor incident as an excuse to break off your relationship."

"It isn't minor. She promised not to keep any secrets. That whatever she discovered she'd tell me."

"She said she would have if Ned didn't, and I believe her," Miranda said simply. "You can't expect her to trust you if you aren't willing to trust her."

She paused. "And here's something else for you to consider. I don't think you're as angry with her as you pretend to be."

"I'm not pretending."

"OK, so you're angry. But Dixie's silence isn't the real reason behind it. You're angry with yourself for not seeing what lay under your nose the whole time. You worked with Ned for six months and didn't suspect a thing, did you? It's easier to make Dixie your scapegoat than to admit your own failings."

He started to protest, then stopped. He couldn't deny that he felt like a complete failure at judging character, but was he blaming Dixie to protect his own ego?

"If you want to spread the responsibility around, then you'd better include Jane and myself. We never suspected a thing either, and we worked with him every day, like you did. Believe me, if I'd entertained even the slightest inkling that he was pickling himself every night, I would have told you."

Mark remained silent.

"Let me give you one last opinion. Letting Andrea go was tough, but you survived. If you send Dixie packing, you'll be sorry for the rest of your natural-born days."

Mark rose, unwilling to admit that he felt Dixie's loss keenly after only twenty minutes. "I need some air."

Miranda nodded. "Good thinking. Maybe freezing your butt outside will cool off your hotheadedness."

He glared at her, irritated that she simply glared back. "As soon as I get back, I'll expect my patients to be lined up and ready to go."

"Impossible."

"What do you mean?"

"Jane and I rescheduled your morning appointments."

"Why did you do that?"

"You didn't need the town as your audience," she said. "When things got hot and heavy, we told everyone to come back this afternoon."

Unsure if he should scold Miranda or thank her, Mark strode down the hallway, intent on reaching his private entrance. He didn't take his coat—he only intended to stay outside until his body to grew as numb as his emotions. Maybe then he could function for the rest of the day...for the rest of his life.

Approaching Dixie's office, he dared himself not to notice the floral scent that always hung in the air. Determined to stride by without giving the occupants a second glance, he started past, then froze at the harsh words being spoken.

"I don't understand how you could have screwed things up," Ned informed Dixie.

Dixie stared at her cousin, incredulous. "How *I* screwed

things up?'' she said. ''I had nothing to do with you walking away from the practice without a word, stealing Mark's money, or refusing to be honest when you *did* come back.''

''I wasn't stealing. I was *borrowing*.''

''Borrowing without permission is stealing,'' she said. ''You're a smart man. You should know the difference.''

''I was going to pay it back.''

''With what?''

''I intended to borrow it from you. Once the shrinks finished my evaluation, I was going to come home and replace the money before anyone knew it was gone.''

''But you didn't get out, did you?''

''No. I was a little worried when I realized I was stuck in Seattle, but I hoped you'd come to the rescue.''

''Yeah. Just call me Dixie Do-right,'' she muttered sarcastically to herself.

''And when Mom told me that you were here, I knew you wouldn't let me sink.''

''Do you know what's really sad, Ned?'' Dixie said, feeling as disgusted with herself as she was with him. ''Until ten days ago, I wouldn't have. For the record, I bailed you out as much as possible.''

''How?'' he demanded.

''Mark was ready to fire you on the spot and I convinced him to listen to your side of the story before he decided your fate.''

''He didn't listen, though, did he?''

''Yes, he did,'' she said hotly. ''If you hadn't spouted off about helping underprivileged people in Mexico when he knew you weren't there, he would have given you a second chance.''

''Mark would have given you a second chance,'' he sing songed in a falsetto voice. ''He certainly would have if you'd paid him off like Mom asked you to.''

''I did, but he gave it back.''

''Then you should have paid him something else.'' Hi

eyes turned speculative. "As friendly as you two are, maybe you did."

"What are you implying?"

"On second thoughts, you can't have been quite good enough. Maybe if you had been, he would have been more lenient."

So incensed was she by his crude comment, she slapped him. Her hand burned from the force she'd applied, but her heart hurt far worse. Did Mark think along those same lines? That she'd spent her days and nights with him as a form of bribery?

Had he lumped her in the same category as his former fiancée, the one who had only been interested in using him to further her own needs?

She wanted to yell at Mark for jumping to the wrong conclusion, but he wasn't in front of her. Ned was.

"How dare you?" she snarled. "Our relationship was something special. Quite unlike yours with Larissa. I love Mark Cameron, so don't you dare say another word. About him or me...or anything. Now, get out. I'll stop by the house to pack up my things and then I never want to see you again."

She'd lost the one man she'd ever loved. The loss of a family who'd never loved her paled in comparison...

Mark stood still, unable to breathe and definitely unable to move after hearing Dixie profess her love for him.

Miranda's whisper came at his elbow. "Who is she protecting now?"

In that instant everything gelled in his head and in his heart.

He slipped into the room. "I couldn't help but hear you from the hallway, Ned."

Dixie made a small sound in her throat but he didn't glance in her direction. If he saw the pain in her eyes, he'd forget all about Ned—and he didn't want to.

"This is a private conversation," Ned remarked stiffly, his face red from a combination of fury and the handprint on his cheek.

"Can't be too private if you're yelling. And when you yell at the woman I admire and love, you can't expect me to ignore you."

Dixie gasped, but again his gaze didn't waver from Ned.

"How fate gave you a relative like your cousin is completely beyond my understanding. You don't deserve her. Nor do I understand why she's knocked herself out all these years to gain your acceptance.

"So I suggest you do exactly as she said. Get out and stay out of our lives until you get your act together."

Ned stormed past. Neither of them spoke until a door slammed in the distance.

"What did you mean by 'our' lives?" she asked softly.

"Just what I said. I don't want him in our lives. Until he turns into a decent human being," he added. "And the way he's going, that may take until the next century."

Her giggle suddenly turned into a sniffle and her eyes became suspiciously moist. "How much did you hear?"

"Enough."

She smoothed her hair with a shaky hand. "Does this mean you're not angry with me any more?"

He stepped close enough to touch her. "A smart and savvy woman told me that I was taking my anger with myself out on you. After you broke all ties with him, I realized how far you'd come and how much you were giving up to stick to your principles."

It seemed tacky to mention how he thought that losing her relatives wasn't any great loss, so he didn't.

"I had no choice," she said simply. "Not if I wanted to live with myself."

Mark took her hands and tugged her closer, pleased that she didn't resist. "I know how much family means to you. Would you be willing to share mine with me?"

"To share yours…? But—"

"You agreed to move in with me," he reminded her.

"That was before all this happened."

. "The offer's still open. Actually, I'm modifying it slightly."

"You are?"

"I want it legal. With a ring and a ceremony and whatever other frills you can dream up."

"Are you asking me to marry you?"

Her eyes glistened. "I don't know what to say."

He stared into those watery depths and hoped she'd see sincerity and love in his. "Say, 'Yes, Mark.' Or 'Whatever date you want, Mark.' Just don't say no."

She smiled, then flung her arms around his neck. "What if I say that I love you?"

"It works for me," he said, clutching her close and sweeping her off her feet. "Because I love you, too."

February 14

Surrounded by friends, Dixie sat at a gaily decorated table in the Hope Community Center and tapped her feet in time to the music. The dance had started a few minutes ago and only a few couples had been brave enough so far to go onto the dance floor, but it wouldn't take long for everyone else to join in the spirit of the evening. For herself, she could hardly wait to be in Mark's arms, even if all they did was stand in one spot and sway to the beat.

She glanced at the rest of the people there. Like the other women, she was wearing the fanciest dress she could find. In her case, it was a beaded red sheath that sparkled under the lights. She'd never felt more like a princess than she did at that moment.

Actually, it wasn't the dress that caused her to feel that way. Mark's admiring gaze did that all on its own.

He had never looked better either, in his dark suit and bow-ie. No one else in the room held a candle to him and the room was filled with men who, as Miranda and her sister Mary had observed "cleaned up rather nicely."

Trying to be heard over the noise of the band and the other

party-goers, Dixie leaned over to speak in his ear. "This turned out better than I'd expected."

He clutched his chest melodramatically. "You actually doubted our ability to throw a party? Just wait until you see what comes next."

As if on cue, the music stopped and suddenly the band's leader spoke into the microphone. "This next song is for all you lovebirds out there. Before we start, we want to recognize one special pair."

Immediately, several spotlights clicked on. Their beams scanned across the crowd before all three focused on Dixie and Mark.

Slightly embarrassed by the attention, she nudged him. "What's going on?" she asked.

He placed a small velvet box on the table in front of her. "Open it."

She knew what rested inside without looking. Too caught up with emotion, she could only say, "Oh, Mark."

"I asked you to marry me a short time ago," he said, "but you never gave me an answer."

She smiled at him, aware of the complete silence as everyone tried to listen to their conversation. "I thought I did."

He shook his head, his gaze intent. "You never said the magic words."

She flipped back the lid to reveal a huge solitaire engagement ring that sparkled under the intense lights. "Yes, please," she said primly as she held out her hand.

With a wide smile that stretched from ear to ear, he slid the ring onto her finger. The crowd erupted into cheers and catcalls, but Dixie hardly noticed because Mark was kissing her.

Justin abruptly pulled her to her feet as the band struck up a romantic ballad. "Come on. You'll have plenty of time for that later."

Before she realized what he was doing, he, Jared and Gale were pushing them onto the dance floor. People formed a circle around them, as if waiting for them to start.

Mark held out his arms. Without hesitation, she placed her right hand in his left, her left hand on his shoulder, and followed his lead as he moved to the music.

Words seemed trite and she simply relaxed against him and gave herself up to his guidance. To her surprise, she discovered that she wasn't as rusty as she'd thought.

More importantly, she realized that everything she'd been searching for, everything she'd ever wanted, she had discovered right here, in a town where hope was more than just a name.

0205/03b

MILLS & BOON®

Live the emotion

_Medical
romance™

THE DOCTOR'S PREGNANCY SURPRISE by Kate Hardy

(London City General)

Dr Holly Jones has never recovered from the shock of losing David Neave's baby — nor from the way he disappeared from her life. Years later they find themselves working together in A&E, and as their long-held secrets come bubbling to the surface they begin to renew their very special bond. Until Holly discovers she's pregnant again!

THE CONSULTANT'S SECRET SON by *Joanna Neil*

Dr Allie Russell is managing the best she can — juggling her work in A&E and Search & Rescue with her two-year-old son. Then Nathan Brewster arrives back in her life as the new A&E consultant. He doesn't know he's Matty's father, and Allie wants to keep it that way. But as she and Nathan draw closer again, it's only a matter of time before he discovers the truth!

NURSE IN RECOVERY by *Dianne Drake*

Charge nurse Anna Wells's life has been shattered by an accident. She needs someone very dedicated and special to help her put the pieces back together... someone like brilliant Rehabilitation doctor Mitch Durant. But Mitch is burnt out, the last thing he needs is another patient — until he sees Anna and realises she's a challenge he just has to take on...

On sale 4th March 2005

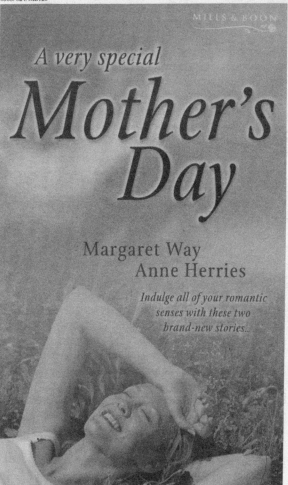

FREE

4 BOOKS AND A SURPRISE GIFT!

We would like to take this opportunity to thank you for reading this Mills & Boon® book by offering you the chance to take FOUR more specially selected titles from the Medical Romance™ series absolutely FREE! We're also making this offer to introduce you to the benefits of the Reader Service™—

- ★ **FREE home delivery**
- ★ **FREE gifts and competitions**
- ★ **FREE monthly Newsletter**
- ★ **Books available before they're in the shops**
- ★ **Exclusive Reader Service offers**

Accepting these FREE books and gift places you under no obligation to buy; you may cancel at any time, even after receiving your free shipment. Simply complete your details below and return the entire page to the address below. You don't even need a stamp!

YES! Please send me 4 free Medical Romance books and a surprise gift. I understand that unless you hear from me, I will receive 6 superb new titles every month for just £2.69 each, postage and packing free. I am under no obligation to purchase any books and may cancel my subscription at any time. The free books and gift will be mine to keep in any case.

M5ZEE

Ms/Mrs/Miss/Mr......................................Initials ....
BLOCK CAPITALS PLEASE

Surname ....

Address ....

....

....Postcode ....

Send this whole page to:
The Reader Service, FREEPOST CN81, Croydon, CR9 3WZ

WIN a romantic weekend in PARiS

To celebrate Valentine's Day we are offering you the chance to WIN one of 3 romantic weekend breaks to Paris.

Imagine you're in Paris; strolling down the Champs Elysées, pottering through the Latin Quarter or taking an evening cruise down the Seine. Whatever your mood, Paris has something to offer everyone.

For your chance to make this dream a reality simply enter this prize draw by filling in the entry form below:

Name _____

Address _____

_____ Tel no: _____

Closing date for entries is 30th June 2005

Please send your entry to:

Valentine's Day Prize Draw
PO Box 676, Richmond, Surrey, TW9 1WU

Terms and Conditions

1. Draw open to all residents of the UK and Eire aged 18 and over. No purchase necessary. To obtain a copy of the entry form please write to the address above. All requests for entry forms from this address must be received by 31st May 2005. One entry per household only. 2. The offer is for one of three prizes of two nights free accommodation in Paris for two adults sharing a twin or double room and based on flights and accommodation being booked as a package. Flights cannot be booked separately or arranged through any other travel company or agent, and are dependent on availability. Holiday must be taken by 31st December 2005. Restrictions on travel may apply. 3. No alternatives to the prize will be offered. 4. Employees and immediate family members of Harlequin Mills & Boon Ltd are not eligible. 5. To be eligible, all entries must be received by 30th June 2005. 6. No responsibility can be accepted for entries that are lost, delayed or damaged in the post. 7. Proof of postage cannot be accepted as proof of delivery. 8. Winners will be determined in a random and independently supervised draw from all eligible entries received. 9. Prize winner notification will be made by letter no later than 14 days after the deadline for entry. 10. If any prize or prize notification is returned as undeliverable, an alternative winner will be drawn from eligible entries. 11. Names of competition winners are available on request. 12. As a result of this application you may receive offers from Harlequin Mills & Boon Ltd. If you do not wish to share in this opportunity, please write to the data manager at the address shown above. 13. Rules available on request.